CHIMP SUPREMACY

The Chimp Supremacist's Handbook

Clifford E. Lewin

authorHOUSE®

AuthorHouse™
1663 Liberty Drive
Bloomington, IN 47403
www.authorhouse.com
Phone: 1 (800) 839-8640

Published by AuthorHouse   10/30/2015

ISBN: 978-1-5049-4841-8 (sc)
ISBN: 978-1-5049-5356-6 (e)

Print information available on the last page.

This book is printed on acid-free paper.

CONTENTS

A Chimp Civilization Begins

Where to begin? Cliff, here. I'm the hero, sort of, of this story. Or at least, it's my story. True, as best I know.

I was at home, turned into a chimp breeding farm, and amateur research lab. Watching yesterday's game film. I already did run thru it once, and now once again, stopping at parts. This morning, yes the sun is already up, I need to get some sleep soon. And wake up soon enough to shave and bath, in time to see my chimps, and my sign language trainer. On the video I was back winding and studying again, was something I needed to see again. "We" (of course I identify with my bros) we're already down 23 to 2. In "Da Chimps"[1] defense, all 23 points the hoomies scored were penalty shots. We still needed to work on that. But my little buddies learn pretty well from films. ...

---

[1] I saw no reason for a more imaginative team name than that. That's what everyone would be calling them, anyway.

Imagine a typical high school gym. 5 chimps wearing muzzles [2], squaring off center of court, for the free throw. V. the high school team. Far from a great high school team. A country school, everyone bussed to a small town. Only one of the 5 on court was black. The ball was tossed to up! The black hoomy had just enough height, reach and leaping ability, to barely tip the ball. It ended up in a blond hoomy's hands. All that kid had going for him, was height and shooting ability. But less that a half second later, a chimp also had 2 hands on the ball. Only 105 pounds, and his feet weren't even on the ground. But he had plenty enough strength to snatch the ball out of the kid's hands. The chimp was Barney! That was a break for us. With any luck, Barney wouldn't get caught double dribbling. Barney was hemmed in on the right side of our goal's half-court. And this dribbling thing, sure does slow down a chimp's superior speed and quickness. Barney panicked and took a shot from 15 meters off. He hit the backboard, which was pretty good for him [3]. One chimp was already holding

---

[2]   Barely necessary. Those chimps, were more civilized, and non-violent, that the average hoomy high school kid. But even high school games can turn into brawls. And chimps are no joke in close quarter combat. They could remove their muzzles in 15 seconds flat. But that would be plenty of time to restore order.

[3]   At the time, the chimps couldn't even shoot baskets as well as I can. To wit, their shooting sucked. It seems, chimp's superior strength does not apply to throwing, and throwing accuracy.

onto the rim with one hand. Which would have gotten us a penalty, if the ref had noticed. The dangling chimp missed the ball. So did a white hoomy, who leaped for it. It bounced into the hands of a chimp who was waiting there out of indecision, not strategy. He threw the ball, and scored a basket. Except the whistle blew. ...

The whistle. That's what I was looking for. When the kid, who leaped for the ball, came down to the floor, he landed square on top of a chimp, who was crouching there, perfectly still. The poor kid hit the floor hard! Plenty of bruises, and some strained knee tendons, that took 2 weeks to heal. Not culpable. In fact, the ref could have opted to penalize the kid. But I knew what Greg did. Greg was completely unhurt. You can't hurt a chimp much, with much less than a good lick with a baseball bat. Actually a clever move. But nor against high school kids! Save moves like that, for when we play an exhibition match with an NBA team. I don't like those over paid, over aged, children, running around in over sized adult bodies, anyway. It wouldn't be easy, communicating those ideas to 5 chimps. Perhaps, Greg should not play against the kids. ...

While you're imagining. Imagine that the gym stadium style seats were packed with the high school kids. The teachers let them all out of class to watch the game, that afternoon. As much cheering and crowd noise as they made, you'd swear that they were chimps, too. The kids were very good sports. Most of them were cheering for the chimps.

When the game ended, and the embarrassing score was announced, the kids booed and hissed. One of the pretty little cheerleaders demanded that we take off the muzzle of one of the chimps, so she could kiss him. Just on the lips, of course. But the stodgy old principal wouldn't allow it.

I had what was once a typical 40 acre farm. Across from a paved, black top road, 20 or so meters from my house. Further down the road, only bordered my 40, for about 50 meters, was another 20 acre strip. Both were surrounded by 20 foot chain link fences. With 2 strands of barbed wire on top. It was not much of an obstacle to chimps. Although it did serve to keep people and animals out. It did, make the chimps think about it, before they left. And individual chimps, have instincts against traveling too far from their group. Few left, and all came back, because they loved it there. And I steadily expressed my displeasure of their leaving, even for a short while, by withholding treats.

During this time, only my 40 acres was terraformed to orchards, shelters and crude, junk lumber constructed huts. The huts had electric heaters, for the winter. The 20 acres, not so ready for expansion, was overrun with scrub brush. It would take a little bulldozer work, to prepare it to be terraformed. I had it connected with a 10 meter high "bridge". Really, a sort of overpass, built with a combination of logs, planks, and fencing wire; that would have made Tarzan proud. Supported by 2 telephone poles, on both sides of the road. More of an overhead tunnel, than a bridge. Often the chimps crossed over, for more privacy, or a change of scenery.

Soon, the "bridge" became the place that chimps socialized with the local folks. They were often given fruit, and other things, (Like beer!). The locals and my chimps had fun trying out their sign language out on each other.

One night, a few months back, I heard gunshots from the direction of, and seemed close to, the chimp bridge. I heard 2 more gunshots, as I grabbed and back pocketed my .22 Jennings pocket pistol. I scrambled out the door, at a slow run down the edge of the road, keeping on the fence line, trying for some little stealth. I soon saw Lancelot, standing in the middle of the road, squeezing, well jerking, off another shot. Wobbling, obviously staggering drunk. A smaller guy, about my size. White, very nondescript, except very decadent looking, especially in his booze, and who knows what else, bloated face. The rifle he was using was unusual, a pump action .22. Fortunately so muzzle heavy, that it threw his aim off, even more than it already would have been. I broke into a full run, and I am exceptionally fast, down the middle of the road. He was too out of it, to hear my steady <Clomp! Clomp! Clomp!> of tennis shoes approaching him. ...

I noticed about 8 different things, including several chunks of wood, a crumpled coke can, and a half eaten apple, lying on the road. Probably thrown at him by my chimps. I shouldered into his back, and sent him flying, on hands and knees. The gun fired into the air, just before it went spinning about 3 meters (10 feet) onto the road. I was almost as stunned as Lancelot. But I had a lot more presence of mind. By the time he even managed to stand. I already jacked out the shell casing in the chamber, along with maybe 4 bullets, squatted down to gather them, and threw them into the bush on the other side of the road. I threw the gun at Lance's feet. The only thing I said to him that night, was "Don't ever do that again. Not Ever."

I looked up and below the bridge for blood. None. But now, 4 chimps were peeping over logs used as boards, at me. I signed at one named George <You hurt?>. And then pointed to the others, meaning <You hurt?>. They, and 3 more appearing, shook their heads, meaning <No>.

Lancelot was lucky those weren't wild chimps. Wild chimps would have probably have killed him. Not that I'd civilized them much. They were just smarter. Unfortunately, being smart can be a disadvantage when dealing with the stupid. Lancelot would probably have gotten lucky, before he ran out of bullets.

During this, and continuing near to my door, Lancelot followed me, with a loud sometimes shouting, tirade. Little of it was coherent. The only thing I remember, was "I'll get you Cliff, if it's the last thing I do!"

In anywhere near a perfect world, that would have been the end of it. But Lancelot was the nephew or cousin, to several top ruling class folks in the county. He had been neighbors and friends, when I went to high school. But our paths separated to very different. For the last year, he filed at least weekly oral complaints to the Sheriffs Department, against my chimps. Petty theft, prank vandalism. Some real, most drug and booze delusions and hallucinations, some out right lies. I could be wrong, but I think Lancelot started it first. He does have a way of bringing out the worst in people, and even animals.

Lancelot made a report on me, this time. His friend, and me thinks sex partner, Sheriff Squeal, had good enough reasons not to like me. And he was a paid-for toady of the ruling class. Happy to help Lancelot get some payback. (But these days, I'm an honest enough businessman, especially by what passes for corporate morals, these days. An almost-pillar of the community.) Fortunately, my chimps were a hot item with the local news media. Especially the local paper. That paper, did a fair, and truthful article.

I bluffed even to when they cuffed my hands behind my back, for a minute. They backed down, and let me go on my own recognizance. Actually, it wasn't a bluff. I had it arranged with a t.v. reporter, to interview me, and try to film me, if I went to jail. Publicity = free advertising. Finally, after nearly a month, they let me plead out to "petty, misdemeanor theft", for the one thing I admitted to; taking and throwing Lancelot's bullets away. $100 fine. They were tired of looking like donkeys in the local paper. (Interesting. Because cops never get charged for stealing peoples' bullets, when they search people. Just-us I suppose).

But Lancelot stopped making complaints on my chimps. So perhaps, it was the best $100 I ever spent.

During the time I was being persecuted in court. Lancelot came knocking on my door, while I was away. Very drunk, and high on who knows what. Noticing that I was gone, and a window open, he crawled inside. What for, I never did find out. He was the neighborhood informant[4]. So maybe, trying to gather some info, or planting some fake evidence on me, or whatever. Perhaps, to steal something to get high on. Like the 6-pack of beer, he did take. (I kept

---

[4]   Occasionally, I'd thought about making him "magically disappear". But in general, a snitch you know, is just a nuisance. It's the ones you don't know, that do the damage. If one even just leaves, no suspicion, he'll probably be replaced. By one you don't know yet.

it for guests.) Whatever it was, it was probably a drugs etc. induced psycho episode urge. That he probably wouldn't remember, after he slept it off.

One of the outcast chimp gangstas, one of the Little Buckaroos, Obie scampered and told big Buck; in their part sign, part gesture, part chimp chattering, language. By the time Lancelot was out my front door, the Buckaroos were waiting for him. In a dumb attempt to gain favor with me. One, Harley, grabbed his legs as he walked out the door. Lancelot fell down, but he didn't hit my over grown lawn very hard. Obie and Moose grabbed an arm apiece. And Buckaroo started ripping his clothes off, torn rag, by torn rag. He set aside everything Lancelot was carrying. Including Lancelot's knife, bag of pot, and the 5 beers left of the 6-pack. Once Lancelot was completely naked, Buckaroo had his way with him. And it wasn't just a leg hump. Moose was about to get his turn, when an old Chevy, brakes screeching, swerved into my lawn, brakes off, gas to the floor, leaving a mud track behind them. Stopping with a jerking, rocking, stop, a meter or two from Lancelot. (Hey! In my hood, even the old ladies think they are racecar drivers.) The doors flew open. And 2 old ladies ran out, swinging their purses like Viking warriors. They never landed a blow. The chimps ran away too fast. Only Harley managed to grab the now 5-pack. Over the fence they scampered. One old lady's swing missed Harley by 6 inches. …

Amazing, that the Sheriffs Department didn't hear about that, too. At least, not until half the county already heard about it. Perhaps Lancelot was too embarrassed. Maybe he liked it.

I decided to search the Internet, and get all the info I could on faggotry. Especially, in chimps. But what was there, was not very useful. Even my computer genius, play-by-mail (p.b.m.) gaming buddy, Hiro couldn't find much of real use, for me. Too much PC, lies and contradictions. (I hope none of you are dumb enough to believe they are born with female brains.) I put out the ads to sell the Buckaroos. But the locals, and anyone within 100 miles, knew better. Over the Internet, I usually only made sales every several months or so. When demand finally meets my high prices. Chimp buying and selling, is a small, if international, community. So I guess, everyone realized my half price offer on 4 chimps, had a reason behind it.

Then, after reading Laverne's report, some mysterious professor, or higher, cancelled my effort to sell the Buckaroos. He wanted a study done on them. Because male faggotry is so rare in wild chimps. So, I could only keep my grant, if I kept the Buckaroos. Me thinks, that still unknown professor is a pervert, himself. The "study" came to nothing. I and Laverne refused to do it. And nobody got around to ordering a grad, or undergraduate, student to do it.

THE DEALER'S WILD

Back from my revelries, to where I chose to begin this novel. Normally, I keep good daylight hours. But that night, I was up to 3 a.m., viewing the game film, and planning tomorrow's lesson. So, when a knock sounded on my front door, at the uncivilized hour of 7 a.m., I barely woke up. Owning a 3 bedroom+ home, inherited, I took to using the living room as if a hotel room. Complete with bed. (A slight help to my sex life. And my sex life needs all the help it can get.) In spite of being 4 meters from the front door, I barely focused to see it. By a heroic effort, I focused well enough to see my alarm clock. 7:03. Much earlier, than the 8ish o'clock, that Laverne would show up. Ah! Laverne. Now that was a buxom blonde fox. Still, probably her. Anyone else, I would of told to come back later. Much later. But Laverne had to drive over 40 miles, to come and teach my chimps, and me, sign language. Something like a minute later, I managed to put on some gym shorts, and a tee shirt, and flicked on the window air conditioner. Mid summer, the room was already mid 80s (Fahrenheit). …

As I walk to the door, there was much louder knocking. Wham! Wham! Wham! I was beginning to think it probably wasn't Laverne. That was, probably, not like her. And by now, I would have heard some giggling. And likely, some inane, but warm and bubbly jabber. But then, again, who could it be? I dreaded this. I wasn't in the mood for warm and bubbly. …

I opened the door and saw six tall, over 6 feet, men wearing JC Penney's suits. I recognized the cut. . I owned one (only) myself. One said "Can we come in Mr. Atreides", as I opening my mouth. "Who are you?" "We are from a federal government agency." "F.B.I.? D.E.A.? What?" As they gently barged in, the spokesman answered "No. We are a different part of the government. But we brought a couple of U.S. Marshals, in case we need some civilian help." Well, it might not have been gentle. If not that I instinctively jumped out of the way. The first one was about 250 pounds of muscle, and only 50 pounds of lard added. The other 5 weren't much smaller. I said ruefully "Well. Now that you're in here, what can I do for you?" I noticed that those suits looked hot. So, being the gentleman that I am, I turned off the AC. ☺ I guessed from their army style, but not buzz, haircuts, clean shaven, they were some flavor of Military intelligence. Or perhaps, 4 different flavors.

They were all non-descript, except for their size, brown hair and eyes. The Marshals were easy to pick out. One had a handle bar moustache. The other was a little bit longish in the hair. "Have you heard the news about the escaped chimpanzee, Mr. Atreides?" ...

I remembered a few articles, that only someone in an animal handling business, would pay attention to, or even read. One thing did get the public attention. A chimp robbed a Junior Food store. And when the cashier tried to give him fruit, instead of money, the chimp shot a bullet into the counter. I caught a lot of teasing about that. Even some real suspicion. ...

They told me: This chimp, they were looking for, was an escapee from a secret government lab. A dangerous, genetically engineered military weapon, that went insane, and has already killed a lot of people. They were shocked that I had 385 chimps, simply running around loose on 60 acres of orchard land. They asked me to help them. We discussed chimp things, and got along famously. I even turned the AC back on. Well, mostly because I was beginning to sweat myself. They asked me to round up all of my chimps. ...

I told them there was only one good way. But unless they wanted to wait until evening, it would cost them $60. Actually, I fed the chimps 3 times a day. And it was already a little late for breakfast. But business was struggling a little worse than usual. So I took advantage. They paid so quick, a nice government check, from their own checkbook, "Treasury Department", that I wished I'd asked for at least double that.

We all walked thru my once family kitchen, that now doubles for a chem lab, and onto the back porch. Which was made of old pine lumber, many boards needing replaced. I rang a ship's type bell, dangling to the side of the 3 porch steps. Which were bare cement slabs, piled on top of each other. Hundreds of chimps leaped into view, over, under, and thru, the 3 strand barbed wire fence, that marked, what passed for my back yard, about a half acre. All of them were there, in less than 5 minutes. I think I had bananas, apples, welfare oatmeal [5], and 4 sugar cubes apiece [6], that day.

---

[5]   Originally oatmeal was their main staple. But as my orchards produced better and better, and they learned to hustle food from the hoomies, they ate less and less of it. To make sure none of them went hungry, I still made plenty of it. A lot of it, was often fed to a neighbor's hogs.

[6]   My chimps had more sophisticated tastes in sweeter-then-fruit than sugar cubes. But I was making a lot of hard economic choices. Besides, the chimps were given, and often traded for, a lot of candy bars, from the "bridge". (I did restrict them to lowering buckets from the bridge. I very insisted that they act like my fence was a serious barrier. Especially around hoomies.) Frankly, my opinion was, that my chimps lived better than most

Once I lugged out their food, in 4 piles, I only supervised. I put it on a long serving table, that was shaded with a tent like tarp. They formed a nice orderly line. So many, that they gave off a musty, only a little unpleasant smell. (I had been conditioning them to bathe, and even swim. But it was early in the day, for that.)

I held up 4 fingers. With only a little chattering, none of the hoots and barks you hear when they are arguing. 4 emerged from the masses. And stood serving behind the tables. While the others walked thru it, and received their food. I already had the items, and portion, set on the table. The servers had learned that. I did not choose who served. The chimps did. I only chose who did NOT serve[7]. I only paid the servers one extra banana. I think, their status was more important. Yet I noticed that there was always 1 to 4 alpha males, who did not deign to serve food. They were already forming a humanesque 3 class system, upper, middle, and "working" class.

---

hoomies anyway. So perhaps, I didn't have enough sympathy for them.

[7] Those that served too much, or too little, or even acted too silly more than once, were also sold. Some had to be sold. That's what kept my precarious business afloat. I resented having to sell so many. That was interfering with my selective breeding of superior chimps. Not that any of my chimps were, knowingly, sold "down the river". And chimps, who are already socialized, know a little sign language, are too high priced to be abused.

"Is this all of you chimps?" asked the apparent leader. A non-descript guy, about as much muscle as their human battering ram, but only about 10 pounds of lard. What there was of his hair, was dark brown, salt and pepper. "It should be." I answered, "Three hundred and eighty five. They rarely miss a meal." "Can you make them stay for a while?" "That depends on how long, and how bad, I want them to stay." "Oh, Mr. Atreides, you want them to fully, cooperate with us, absolutely bad. Your business, and maybe even a few years of your freedom, depends on it. What we need from you is two things. One. We need your chimps to stay right here, while a special military team searches your farm for the escaped chimp. Two. We need to take a small blood sample from all of your chimps, except the very youngest. Some very important people, want to be absolutely sure, that none of your chimps are the escaped murderer." …

I laughed, "This is going to be harder than you think. Most of my chimps are needle shy. Hmmmm. Send one of these guys up to that gas station, country store, you saw when you turned off this road, Padgett's Trading Post. Buy every candy bar, candy and fruit they have. Bribes to pacify. And don't even think about starting with the needles, until my sign language instructor, Laverne[8], gets here. She's much better at communicating with them, than I am. There probably isn't enough loot at the store. So she'll have to negotiate for you. Don't worry, she'll translate it into a check."

As I was speaking, the leader, "Tom" he said, pulled out a cell phone. Seconds after I said that, he was giving orders. Over 120 elite soldiers of some type, who already had my property surrounded from a distance, came into the open. And surrounded the fences up close. Looking hyper alert, and homicidal.

To me, he barked "Please unlock and open that gate We do not want to damage any of your property." I did so. The swing gate was 8 feet high, 12 feet wide, a light iron pipe frame, with chain link fence on the frame. A simple chain and padlock locked it. As I did this, 4 death commandos ☺ seemed to appear out of nowhere, watching that suddenly open entrance. Harmless, enough, M-16s up in the air at about 45 degree angles. Like all the rest, they were wearing army BDU uniforms, with zero insignia, adornment etc.

---

[8] I'm part of a University of Alabama scientific research grant. Sort of like the tail wagging the dog. But that's the way I worked past all the politics and elitists' privilege. What I got was, $2000.00 every 3 months, the lovely Laverne visiting my chimps and me, teaching us sign language, usually twice a week. And over 100 students and professors studying us, and advising me. (Not that all that meddling was particularly useful.)

Not a word. Not a smile. Expressions that couldn't quite be called frowns.

As the gate was wide opened, a non-descript, dusty, tinted glass, white van stopped in front of my house. After a few seconds stop, it turned into my yard, about 20m.p.h., and thru the gate. It slowed to a halt, at the clearest area it could find.

4 army clothed nurses took a folded, then unfolded, table out of the van. And neatly on the table, assorted medical gear, and needles. Obviously to take blood with. And a cubish looking, maybe 1 meter cubed, white, refrigerator. I guessed it to run on battery power. No plug. The four 20ish year old nurses were actually fairly pretty. But that didn't quite register on the senses. Not with the frumpy army clothes, semi-butch hair cuts, and painted on, plastic, half smiles.

About that time Laverne showed up, her usual 30 seconds to 5 minutes early. Now there's a girl that knows how to dress and appear sexy, while still being completely lady like. Comfortable pants and blouse. Very blonde, tall, many curves. A cute, pointed, barely too large, nose on a classic beautiful face. She is also strongly built. Although not really noticeable, except a little in the legs. Quite the athlete, mainly a distance runner. (Needless to say, I never got anywhere at all, trying to seduce, or even date, her.) Laverne had nothing to do with with whatever college degrees cover chimpology. She was a psych major. She even managed to graduate, in spite of me, and my chimps. Her over-riding qualification, was that she was much better at sign language, than any of the other more than 20 candidates. She also brought her cat, her several dogs, her cockatoo, and a goat to her first interview, to demonstrate how good she was with animals. (Not that when the time came, for me to pick from their 3 finalists, that her qualifications were an issue.) ☺

Laverne loves to giggle. And when she does, everyone else starts giggling too. Everyone. Even me, who has a well-known reputation as impassive and poker faced. It would not shock me to learn, that it's truly a magic power.

The first I noticed of her, was her smile. Sort of like the Cheshire cat, it appears first, and disappears last. Usually, her giggling gives her away, before she does that. I guess she was too shocked by all the strange sights and happenings, to do that. But her giggles, weren't far behind. "<Giggle! Giggle! Giggle!>" "What have you been doing?! Teaching my chimps how to rob banks?! <Giggle>" I stage whispered "Laverne! We need to talk." I pulled her aside, by the hand, in a far corner of the 3 strand barbwire fence, away from the feds. I quickly explained the sitz, and offered "Negotiate a big price, and I'll split it with you."

When we came back to the clutter of feds and chimps, around the nurses' table. Leader/Tom asked me very suspiciously, "What was that about?" Laverne answered "<Giggle! Giggle!> You're going to write us both big identical checks! <Giggle! Giggle!> " Yes, even the feds, eventually, giggled with her.

As soon as the first 120 death commandos had a secure perimeter around my farm. Another around 120 stormed the fence near the paved road, with a very long, awkward ladder. As soon as it was resting nearly a vertical climb, several climbed up on it. And drug a second identical ladder, already fully extended, up, and over. It thudded on the ground, on the other side. They quickly lashed the 2 ladders together. Up, over, and down they trooped. And searched my farm very thoroughly. "Hammer and anvil" sweeps, and shrinking circles. It didn't take them long, to do a perfect job. Especially with infrared (body heat) detecting devices, to scan the trees, in my fairly well kept up, chimp maintained, orchards. Which had little underbrush ect.

Tom/Leader got a call on his cell phone. He mumbled into it. Waited. Mumbled again. "Out!" He waved his pack of feds over. They had a mumble session. Then he ordered "O.K. Start taking blood samples." Then to me, a near whisper "Mr. Atreides. We need to speak to you again. As soon as you can be spared." "Laverne. You can handle this, can't you?" "Sure", she winked and giggled. Tom/Leader ordered the remaining Marshal, "Keep a watch on things out here."

I walked through the back door, with the feds, and noticed 4 death commandos sitting on my chairs and couch in my living room. Casual posture, not near as homicidal looking, but still hyper alert. Apparently, they were there to guard against any chimp exiting from my house. I flipped on the air conditioning to max, to make up for lost time. Finally seeing the sense in being a decent host, I put 2 mugs, and 3 plastic glasses in the micro nuker. I laid out my ad hoc coffee and flavorings etc., 5 spoons, on the table.

Tom/Leader started the discussion. "The killer chimp isn't here. And I do not expect us to catch him, until he makes a mistake. Even a normal chimp, would be hard to find and catch, if he's running from us. It might take years. This seemed like the most likely place. From here on out, we'll be making less and less likely guesses. But from all out advisers, he is a social animal. Sooner or later, he'll make friends with humans or chimps. Most likely both. So. It seems more likely than not, that he will show up here some day. So. We will be keeping watch. Very discreetly, every now and then, a few of us will sneak onto your property, no warning, you'll never know. You did hear about the ten thousand dollar reward?" I nodded, and he continued. "We could use your help every now and then.

Friendly, say nothing, courtesy to strangers, let us know of anything suspicious. Maybe an occasional visitor, for coffee," he held up his mug in salute, "when it's really cold or too hot, outside."

I asked "Ten gee is a little small, for how important this guy is. Why wouldn't I just sell him to the communists? Oh! Excuse me, I guess I'm still stuck in the '80's. The Muslims. Or the narcoterrorists. Or whoever, we're currently hating on?" "That would be bad Mr. Atreides." He looked at each of the others, one at a time. 2 shrugged. Dick, as so Leader/Tom had called him, smiled as if in deep thought for a few seconds, and said "You know, boss. This guy COULD pull that off. Clever, and really too brave for his own good." They all looked at each other, for around 10 seconds, not saying anything. Obviously, I'd just stepped into a position, where they were considering making me "magically disappear", and put an agent into my house, to run my business. Running out of the door was not an option. They had guns under their suits. And mine were miles away, in my used to be bedroom.

Fortunately, before my shock wore off, and my legs started to tremble, they got what passes for mellow in these guys. "But I LIKE this guy!" Tom/Leader laughed. "I do too", said He's-Hairy-Too, as Tom called him. But he didn't sound very sincere.

Tom/Leader made me an offer. "Frankly Mr. Atreides. We work from a very secret budget. That does not exist. Please! Your nickel and dime bills, are already killing us. Please! No more. Putting you on salary would be a lot of trouble, and worse explaining. Not unless you insist. What we like to deal in, is favors. And I know enough about you, that I know we can do you some very nice favors. You are cash starved. With more money, surely this place could house a lot more chimps. And maybe, you would want to buy more land. It's amazing you made it as far as you did, with your chimp basketball team. You did a good job with the publicity. And in gaining a following in the press. But the NBA is dragging their feet. I think you will finally rope them in. But it could take years. I am going to have to work it thru our business department. But yes – I can! I heard, you did not do well against a weak high school team. Can you be ready to play an NBA team, in 30 days?" "Yes." I said nodding. Actually, I wasn't at all sure. But so what, if we lost by penalty shots. He continued, "I will try. Maybe not in thirty days. But soon. When you are ready to try an NFL football team, I will have a friend on the inside of the Atlanta Falcons call you. But", he smiled predatorily. …

"We are going to want more than your best, and most enthusiastic help, trying to capture the killer-ape. … One. We want an alternate soldier-chimps project. And you're just the man to do it. Simply put, we want to train and sell us chimp soldiers. We are not expecting much, but we do expect you to keep producing better and better soldiers. Of course, like all fed contracts, it will pay very well. Will you do it?" I said blandly, "I could be persuaded." We both smiled. Yes, I could be persuaded, like a starving wolf could by persuaded to eat fresh, raw, meat.

He continued, "Two. We also want forty percent of your entire business profits, after taxes. No funny business. Every penny. Send it to a Swiss bank account, that we'll e-mail you, in a few days." "Ten percent." "No way. Be reasonable. Within six months, you will have more income than a county boy like yourself can spend, without getting foolish or very frivolous. Thirty percent, my last offer." "Twenty percent." "Thirty percent. And. We will use our influence, when needed, to try to save you from any tax trouble you get into. No promises. So do not get carried away. But in any case, you will get max leniency. And you would be wasting money, hiring a tax lawyer to defend you." At that level of income, that was a nice concession. I said "Done!" We all laughed for a minute. Then Tom/Leader said "Well! Let us go outside, and see how things are going. Who knows, maybe the killer chimp is hiding among yours. "I very doubt it." "We shall see. I have to finish this job anyway." …

When we stepped out in my backyard, about half of my chimps had given blood. Bravely, and passively, enough.

It was then, that my worst behaved chimp, Buck, decided to act up. He was my oldest. At least 20 years old, some gray hair. I bought him from a circus, for only $100. They just "wanted someone to give him a good home". That sounded like a great deal to me. He already knew a few tricks. He was socialized and comfortable with people and chimps. A nice elder example for my chimp community. Yea. Right. I should have known better. That circus had already degenerated into more like a carnival. And they no longer needed a dog, a pony and chimp show.) Well. Buck had a little problem. …

Buck had already given blood. But every chimp still had to wait around, anyway. Until they were all declared not killer-chimps. Nobody ever figured out why Buck went crazy. (Well. Crazier than usual.) Maybe, it was the strangeness and stress, of the event. Maybe it was because Harry, the fed battering ram, looked like one of his pervert ex-masters. Maybe, it was because Harry was the biggest mate human there. Anyway. Buck charged, and grabbed a hold of Harry's leg, and started buckarooing. Within a dozen seconds, Harry's pants leg was being slimed with chimp semen. Harry did his enraged best to rip Buck off his leg. (And do who knows what, after that.)

But chimps have superhuman strength. And their feet count almost as much as their hands. (Their feet have opposable toes, and fairly strong grips.) Between Harry and Buck, they ripped his pant leg up to his knees. And Buck was still hanging on, and buckarooing.

Laverne was enraged. She punched Buck up side his head, where a human temple would be, with a haymaker. She hits hard! I think, harder than an average dude her size, which isn't all that small. Unfortunately, it hurt her somewhat dainty hand, worse than it hurt Buck. Buck missed a stroke, but he continued buckarooing. She dropped kicked Buck like a football! That was a mistake! Her cute pink girly boots were hard for girly boots. But not hard enough. Fortunately, she connected with Buck's neck instead of his head. Even so, she was jumping up and down, holding her foot, for a moment. But that loosened up Buck's grip just enough, that Harry managed to rip him loose, and then threw him against my solid wood tool shed. Buck staggered off, slipped thru the 3 strand barbed wire fence, and into the orchards. His head was lolling slightly to the side, from Laverne's kick. His young chimp following, the Buckaroos, Obie, Moose, and Harley, snarled and bared their teeth, and wicked eye tooth fangs. But being cowards, they followed behind Buck, with no trouble.

Of course, none of my chimps was the killer chimp. Things finally settled down. Everyone left. Leaving me alone. To plan for these new opportunities.

THE SPACE RACE

This is the body of an e-mail, I sent to Hiro, a play-by-mail gaming friend of mine.

"Quit your $10,000 a month suit-and-tie job, to form your own moon colony company!?! I admire your courage and boldness. If not your wisdom. ☺ If it falls thru, you can always hang around here, until you get another job. What's another hominid to feed? I hope you like bananas, and living in trees. ☺"

Thank for your offer to buy chimps from me. I, for one, think p.b.m.ers should network together and help each other. It makes me feel real good that you offered. Normally, I'd snap up your offer, like a big bass. But I don't think you researched that angle, near as well as you researched the rest. You do NOT want to use chimps as part of the initial colonists. In spite of never seeing you face to face, I think we're pretty good friends. So I do not want to sell you chimps, that I know you only think you want. (I know you wouldn't do that to me either.) …

(1) Chimps aren't smart enough to substitute for hoomies. With the outrageous shipping expenses. My understanding is that cargo will have a "freight cost", of more than its weight in gold. (Although your theories of reducing that, sound very workable to me.) In spite of being a chimp supremacist ☺, I must say your best will be hoomies. (2) Even my own chimps are not as socialized as hoomies. Worse than little children. Especially the males, often have violent and destructive temper tantrums. (3) As long as it's been since the 1st men on the moon. I don't think it'll be all that risky, anyway. Besides, as a gamer, you ought to know not to increase the risk of the mission failing, than to make things a little safer for the passengers. Anybody going to the colony should be an adventurer of some sort. And taking risks is what adventures DO.

If you want a mascot or a pet, or just one to stay on earth, to help attract publicity and attention. Then, I'll be happy to give you one. The publicity should benefit me, at least as much as its price would have, anyway.

However, if you do come up with some practical use for my chimps, I sure could use the money! Still struggling here.

Yes, treating the project like mainly a marketing and sales problem, is both brilliant and simple. Sounds like a winner to me! Surely you can come up with "just" 150 one hundred+ millionaires to invest, for an assortment of reasons. Perhaps, they don't want to go themselves. But I think that many would want to send a son or daughter, to spread their genes thru out the galaxy. Yes I (and most scientists) agree, the moon is an ideal space base. An orbiting space station certainly isn't.

I very agree, a one page ad in "U.S.A. Today" is a good idea. Gain the right attention, and establish legitimacy and seriousness. But I bet you won't get it. Not with N.A.S.A. and their allied "pork barrel" brothers against you.

I know Nevada isn't exactly famous as a farm state. So, I'm going to comment on agriculture on the moon. Once you finally get rolling. Lots smarter, and more knowledgeable on their subjects, than I, will be giving you all kinds of apparently good advice. But most, will be trying to sell you products or agendas. I hope you know I'm good for non-partisan advice. Actually, your partisan. ...

Everyone will be trying to sell you grow-lights. And they might be a good idea at first. But it will slow your expansion, if dependent on earth, for replacements. And I'd guess that manufacturing them, will be hard to set up. I don't see them as necessary nor desirable. True, the moon's sunlight will kill plants. But that can be filtered via a special tinted glass roof. That would call for a powerful cooling, or heat transfer, system. Because on the moon, it's either a lot of sunlight, all the time, or none. Alternately, I would bet that fiber optics could both carry, and filter, the sunlight to elsewhere. Possibly, more practical.

Their 1st serious ag. product will likely be mushrooms. No need for sunlight.

Don't let anyone sell you on hydroponics. (l) Water is the biggest potential bottleneck of your expansion. In a recycled water sitz, hydroponics would tie up a lot more water, than basic soil based agriculture. (2) Extracting nutrients would make that cost a lot of labor etc. (3) Like it or not. A healthy ecology calls for recycled wastes. Just mushrooms, will not do that. Waste not, import from earth not. (4) I see no point in implementing hydroponics, even during the start. Why so much labor, and earth imports, into a project that will eventually be scrapped, or very limited? Simply importing food from earth, at first, makes more sense. Not wasted. Humans readily convert it into the sort of fertilizer best suited, to enhance sterile moon soil, to productive soil. ... Of course, food production is not the moon's forte. But mostly self--sufficiency should be strived for. Especially, to stay independent of earth.

The first "food" animal should be worms. A practical necessity, to convert soil. They ARE edible and nutritious. Surely, creative cooks can make them palatable, to the less squeamish. We should strive to eliminate that food prejudice from the second generation colonists.

Worms are necessary, to add more necessary animal protein, to chickens' diet. Chicken eggs are one of the most efficient ways to produce animal protein. (Second to milk cows. Which, alas, are very impractical on the moon. Perhaps after a few years, a few milk goats would be an affordable luxury.)

The most efficient commonly accepted meat animal is the rabbit. Red meat. Very suited for the moon's sitz. Not popular in modern times, because of the labor needed to butcher a rabbit. But even to have the ag. self-sufficiency to resist an earth embargo, it will take about 10% of the workers in ag. (Note the rabbit furs. And that around half the rabbits, separated, should be fur rabbits.)

Well. This is getting long. I have an idea that is probably better than copying earth, for moon made solar energy panels. But, I expect earth imported panels will be wise, at least for a year after your 1st colonist is there. So, no hurry.

Re: Feudal Lords. Sorry about the blunder! I misscribed from my scratch draft Turn. (By the time the computer got to selling my food to my Townsmen, I'd already sold all my food.)

Consider me a real-world ally on your Moon Colony project. But not as kamikaze, as I sometimes am, in gaming. Admitted, compared to a moon colony, my chimp farm is a kid's ant farm. But I'm just getting rolling. In a few years, I could probably finance a moon colony, using your sales etc. oriented style myself. But my progress is fueled by money. So, please excuse any apparent stinginess in advance. I will do anything reasonable to help. Besides, I, and my chimp buddies, have bad eating habits. ☺

I'm proud of you! … Cliff

Opportunity Knocks

2 days later. Dawn. Knocking on my door. It was one of those days I chose to get up, and watch the sunrise. So, I was very awake. Sipping micro-nuked tea. And contemplating what cereal I was going to use, for my not so famous cliffochino. Puzzled, but not really expecting another fed invasion, I opened the door. And suddenly in the doorframe, was a chimp pointing a .38 at me. I instantly noticed that some (or all) of the chambers had bullets in them. I managed to stay calm. Probably calm enough, that I didn't have the fear scent on me. Except the gun, he didn't seem to be threatening. I calmly and soothingly said, "Take it easy boy", several times, as I signed "Let's sign/talk". The chimp gave a chimp-grin. Signed <Eff That>. Then reached into his backpack with his other hand. I was so tunnel-visioned on the gun, that I hadn't noticed the backpack, even though it was almost as bulky as he was. A large kid's school type.

He fished out, and threw to me, a folded paper. Which I caught. It was hand printed, fairly legible, masculine scrawl.

I don't like sign language. I only have a 700 or so word sign vocabulary. (About 400 words more than mine!) But I write good. And if you speak American English, I understand it very well.

I said, "Put the gun away. Let's talk. I heard about you on the news. I want to help you." The chimp put the gun in his backpack, brought out pen and paper. I said "I'd like to have you as my guest of honor. But we have to be very careful, and smart. The feds just searched this farm two day ago. Please tell me about yourself." I read <The last fed soldiers (?) stopped watching you, yesterday at sunset. But yes, they will be back again. ...>

I already had visions of easy multi-million dollars dancing in my head.

We continued to communicate in slow, but otherwise pretty good style of communication. I gave him a mug of cliffochino[9], while I drank mine. For this occasion, I chose

---

[9]   Drinking a cliffochino is a lot like eating cereal, except: You use a coffee mug instead of a bowl. You mix instant coffee into the milk. Use a cereal of your choice. Perhaps spices, such as cinnamon or chocolate. Once you have eaten the cereal, instead of

frosted flakes. He added 2 teaspoons of sugar. As usual, with the very sweet cereals, I added no sugar. As usual, I added either cinnamon, or my special spice mix, that included real vanilla. Sometimes, I add chocolate powder, instead. Within days, he was addicted.

I don't know if it was the coffee or my magic recipe. He had only tried a small cup of coffee, before. Or perhaps, it was because I explained to him, that in moderation, caffeine did NOT dull the senses. But added energy and alertness. (O.K. O.K. That is the caffeine addict's point of view. There are worse addictions.)

His name is JC. He doesn't know why. Nor what the initials stand for. We speculated that it might be Jesus Christ. Perhaps joking about him being the antichrist. (They did consider him a beast. ☺) My best guess is Julius Caesar. As in Caesar of "The Planet of the Apes". A mystery.

JC's story was a lot different than the news' and government's. I later knew it to be the exact truth. JC was one of 40 chimp genetic engineering results. The others were failures. Several were not viable enough to be kept alive. Some had serious birth defects, none had any more that chimp-average intelligence. JC was the product of an

---

an inconvenient left over milk, you have a nice drink. Poor Man's cappuccino.

error, that the head scientist, White Hair, could only guess at. But with JC, they hit the jackpot. A little over human average intelligence.

JC was to be the starting breeding stock, of a breed of military chimps. A whole team was educating him.

However, White Hair realized how dangerous a weapon the chimps could be. He likened it, to nuclear warfare. And he worried about what would happen, when inevitably the chimps rebelled, and went on their own, knowing nothing except how to kill and pillage. White Hair killed and cremated all the experimental chimps, except JC. Along with all useful records. And dumped all the ashes into the nearest creek. He burned the lab down. And as the first fire truck arrived, he slowly sipped a quart of cheap wine, laced with a hundred times fatal dose of p. cyanide. He knew that he, nor anyone else, could not withstand a fed government "hard ball" interrogation.

Because all the other researchers thought that their lucky result, was caused by their methods. Not a "dumb" mistake, by an assistant. It would be virtually impossible, for the government to produce a super-chimp for, at least, 20 years.

But White Hair loved JC like the son he never had. He knew that JC wasn't evil. Nor was it a bad thing for chimps to have human level intelligence. If, it was in the hands of nature, not the U.S. government.

So, he planned weeks before, and helped JC escape. JC had a list of where most chimps in the U.S. were. But my farm was at the top of the list. Because mine was a breeding farm. And my radical approaches were known among chimp researchers. That is, I was known as a free thinker.

2 weeks later. By now, the weather was getting a little cold for chimps, some days. I had 12 huts, with small electric heaters in them. That I could switch on and off, from my house. The day after JC arrived, I installed one in a run down, falling in, wooden tool shed, about center of my 40 acres. I put in an over-ride switch for JC. And a hidden plug box, so he could add more appliances. To make the JC cottage more difficult to find, his power lines were hidden under the main line, that I had over the ground, raised off the dirt, on bush branches and the like. His line, was buried in standard pvc. electrical pipe. I let him borrow my tools anytime he wanted. And I got him a load of assorted boards, and a selection of nails. I told him to make his home improvements look like normal chimps did it.

He did that perfectly. He made the other chimps do that. It took him less than 48 hours to become the commanding officer of the chimps. Except for the Buckaroos, who seemed very afraid of him.

I and JC were hanging out in my living room. Which was becoming a habit, those days when I didn't have friends or a girlfriend over. We made plans, and all sorts of contingency plans, for good and bad events. We discussed economics and social engineering. And what I euphemistically called "modern martial arts" or "arts of destruction". Both of us were very good at that, but in different ways. We learned a lot from each other. JC often borrowed a book or two of mine. And sometimes asked me to buy him more books.

I also bought him a few, I chose, to round out his rather lopsided, and gapped education. Including a set of Encyclopedia Brits. Which, like all his books, he kept in a hidden hidey hole, in his "cottage's" floor. Because if anyone snooped around looking for him, that would be a big clue.

JC was always ready, and did a few times, go thru my back window, when-someone unexpectedly stopped by. Of course, in back of the house, there were always a few chimps hanging around. Often, when I was doing other things, JC would watch video movies.

This time, we watched 2 "Planet of the Apes" together. I owned, not rented, the whole series. So I could goof with my friends, that those were my favorite movies. I knew that would be a hoot. JC never heard of it. You can bet, that back at the lab, that was on the forbidden list. ☺ I pointed out the chimp rebel, and said "There you are! J. Caesar." JC denied scribbling <No! You're Caesar!> "How do I get to be Caesar?!" <Because you're the chimp who can speak.> We both had a big laugh at that. "JC you know I've been thinking. If we are raided, we'll probably lose. Sooner or later, that will probably happen. And I can come up with only one good way. ...".

I'd liked to have ordered 50 yards of 3 foot inner diameter storm and drainage pipe. But too many people would have noticed that. Instead, I ordered a lot of 2 X 4 boards, and some plywood sheets. And a new buzz saw. (This project would have worn out the cheap plastic one, I already had.) JC had to do a lot of tedious supervising and training, to get my chimps to do most of the work. And that was a lot of work. But we ended up with an underground tunnel, 10 yards from my fence, and 40 yards past it. Under a farmer's corn stalk stubbed field. We did such a good job of replacing grass and corn stalks, afterward, that the farmer would have to had looked pretty close, to notice it. After the first good rain, all signs were gone. It was deeper that plough and disc. We did no opening in the field. It was a use once thing. I did leave two broken handled shovels at the end, so we could make a hole quickly. Similar camouflage in the chimp farm. Including a wild black berry grove around the opening. (Commonly referred to in my 'hood, as briar berries. A very serious deterrent, to the simply nosy.)

Up until this time, I only played and joked about being a chimp supremacist. About one hour after meeting JC, I became a chimp supremacist for real. And more radical all the time. Our chimp supremacy strategy was simple. I bought a lot of female chimps, more than JC could handle. When he couldn't keep up, I broke out the "basting syringe". To keep max gene diversity, I sold each one after one JC baby. The only long timekeepers, were my sports chimps' ladies. And I bred all my, more or less, physically superior sports chimps daughters with JC, at least, via the basting syringe. JC averaged over 40 pregnant chimps a month. Most of which, were not basting syringe babies. The only part JC chimps that I sold, were both 1/16th or less. And, scored mid average or less, for non JCs, on our intelligence, aptitudes, and physical testing composite. JC, or the basting syringe, would also breed with any top quality 1/16ther.

Although we didn't allow the half breeds to breed together. And we limited the quadroons to as few as practical, after the first generation.

Chimp breeding was once my main profit. Now, it was a big loser. To wit, I was now more of a buyer, than a seller.

Here's a math problem for those of you who want one: If; JC breeds 40 chimps a month, for 30 over years. Half of those babies are female, who breed 50% females. They breed at average 10 years old. And average one baby a year, for an average of 23 years. And have an average lifespan of 40 years. And, weigh 110 pds. /50 kilos. How long will it take, before the mass of JC chimps = the mass of planet earth? …

Yes, ours was a quiet, peaceful, revolution. But the devil was in the conflicting details. Frankly, the main problem was, most of your hoomy leadership, were a bunch the unreasonable, super-selfish, violent, warmonger, totally without honor, scumbags.

BUGGEROOS, THUGGEROOS, AND BUCKEROOS

A few days after our escape tunnel was completed. JC was back in my living room, with the spoils from raiding my refrigerator. On his way out, he asked to borrow my video camera. He wouldn't tell me what he wanted to do with it. He wrote that it was a surprise. Now, I've learned to be very not-enthusiastic about chimps' surprises. But JC was different. And the only way I could find out what, was to lend him the camera.

JC brought back the camera 3 days later. Here's what I saw on video.: Someone was videoing a chimp mother, Lucy, who had just brought 2 pears down from a tree. And was about to share with her little son. Suddenly, she was surrounded on all 4 sides, by the Buckaroos. All 4 Buckaroos started hooting and chattering in a mean and predatory sort of way. Moose half grabbed, half slapped, the 2 pears out of her hand. She turned trembling, afraid, but she still snarled at them. With her mouth open, showing wicked fangs. The

Buckaroos snarled back, almost simultaneously. But did no violence. Instead, Obie and Harley each grabbed one of the pears. Harley started eating "his". But with a look from Buck, Obie demurely handed Buck "his" pear. Harley gave Moose "his" pear, when he'd eaten half of it. Obie seemed to think it was an honor, to eat the small bit left of the pear's core, when Buck handed it back to him. While the Buckaroos were eating, the view wobbled a little, like the camera was changing hands.

Moose threw his pear core, which hit Lucy in the forehead. She snarled and showed teeth and fangs again. Trembling with fear, the baby hugged on its mother's legs. She was entangled, and so could not fight very well. Then, the Buckaroos pounced. Buck started pulling the baby from her. While the other 3 started grabbing and biting the mother. Just little nipping bites, that barely drew blood. When she tried for a real chimp bite, that can easily cripple or kill, their hands were all over her. She was as helpless as if she was hog tied and gagged. They continued biting her, and very enjoyed it. They were going into a frenzy. She might have died horribly, the death of a thousand cuts. But JC entered the scene.

JC was carrying a 3 foot long piece of broom handle, with a sheath knife on both ends, tied to it with a lot of iron tie wire. Meanwhile, Buck finished slapping around, and pinching the baby. That didn't seem necessary. The baby had already been terrified and traumatized. But that made Buck very excited. After a few seconds of beating his chest like a gorilla. Buck grabbed the little chimp, and was about to buckaroo him. The only thing that saved the baby chimp for a few more seconds, was he kept instinctively pushing Buck away, as feeble as it was.

If anyone has any doubts, how fagosexuality is spread among chimps or humans, they should watch that video. Buck, a 1st generation fag, molested by pervert hoomies. Who molested his 3 Buckaroos. Who were networking together with Buck, to molest another generation of perverts. On CD ROM.

First Moose, then Obie, then Harley, each jump up, and then tried to jump up again, in mid air. Like something in a cartoon. As JC stabbed one buttock, then another, with his knife-spear. All 3 jumped up and scampered in terror, behind Buck, and started hugging on Buck for comfort. Buck screeched in anger, clawing at his own Buckaroos, frustrated because he was too entangled to buckaroo the baby chimp. Before Buck was even aware JC was around, JC stabbed out Buck's left eye, with a flick of his spear. Then 3 more flicks, faster than a boxer's jab, and 3 bloody cuts appeared around Buck's right eye. Probably just to show Buck, that he could put the other eye out, if he wanted to.

The little baby scampered to his mother, and started hugging her again. But this time, not in terror, but out of love.

JC started spinning the spear around, like it was as majorette's baton. And he jumped into the air, doing a flip. The 3 Buckaroos weren't exactly brave. In fact, they were coward bullies. Turned hopeless cowards, when they were first buckarooed. (Very typical.) But they were stupid, even for chimps. They didn't think weapons give you much of an advantage. Chimps' natural weapons, fang, claw and fist, are very formidable. There was never an adult chimp on my farm, that couldn't kill me in a "fair" fight. In fact, weapons wouldn't have helped the buckaroos much. They had no instincts for them. Their faulty brains came up with an idea, that JC was away from the other chimps. So no chimps would come to JC's rescue, if they ganged up on him. 4 to1! Well, they didn't realize that Buck was out of it, either. So they attacked first.

Meanwhile, Buck was whining and chimp-crying, as he backed away. Lucy was in no shape, at all to fight. But she managed to stand on 4 feet, and even charge Buck like a snarling rabid dog, with the 2 big wicked eye-teeth fangs. But Buck went coward heart, running away, and screeching in fear, to the opposite side of the farm. But momma chimp managed to catch him, before he made a lightning fast 100 meters. Even though, she nearly passed out, did go semi-conscious and collapse on the ground. But not before she bit off most of Buck's right buttock. Buck could have then turned and easily killed her. But Buck was in terror mode. Now pissing, and defecating, as he lurched along on mostly 3 legs.

Meanwhile. JC was making the fight look a lot harder than it was. JC could have beaten all 3 easily, without a weapon. He was still twirling his spear, and even doing an occasional somersault flip. He also kicked the Buckaroos quite a few times. Which is easy for a chimp to do, he was really just punching with his feet. (After watching that video, I told myself I would never let another chimp watch a kung fu movie.) JC only stabbed with his spear, when he had to, to avoid wrestling with the spear. Then, invariably, even the lightest prick, would make the buckaroo back off, shrieking. And looking to see if his Buck brothers were still going to fight, before jumping back in.

Once, when Obie had no help for a few seconds, he even let Obie take his spear. Then, he punched Obie in the face 3 times. They snatched his spear out of Obie's hands, while Obie was totally out of it.

All of this was lighting fast. Like a Kung Fu movie run on double speed.

Finally, as the 3 buckaroos were ready to break and run. (Not much actual damage, considering how physically tough chimps are.) JC glanced at the camera, to make sure it had a good angle. Shrugging his shoulders, and shaking his head, like he was tired of the game. 3 flicks of his spear, faster than a boxer's jab. All 3 Buckaroos stumbled back, holding their right eyes, blood flowing thru their fingers. …

All in all, that was quite a film. Someday I'll market it, and see how many millions I'll make.

By now, a chimp audience was beginning to gather. JC signed <Take her (Lucy) to Cliff.> Several chimps did. Then he signed <Bring the (obscene gesture, meaning Buckaroos) to me.> In spite that the Buckaroos were terrified, they didn't resist. They did urinate and defecate, as they were drug to JC. Except Buck himself, who had no more urine or feces, since his fight with momma chimp, Lucy.

JC signed to the Buckaroos <Never come back, or I kill other eye.> Although the Buckaroos had never learned much sign language, they more of less got the message. JC strolled over to my fence on the roadside, up the road from the "bridge". JC climbed to the top of the fence, straddled it with his legs, so that none of the barbed wire barbs struck him. He signed <Bring, that (Buckaroo) to me.> With a chimp grabbing both his arms, Buck was more drug, then climbing the fence. When he was in reach of JC, JC picked him up over his head, and threw him head down, at the hard ground, on the roadside. Of course, Buck righted himself, and landed on his feet. But a 30 foot fall should even seriously injure a chimp. The other 3 suffered the same fate. They all lived. It seems, they even managed to crawl away under their own power. Or at least, with help from each other.

Lucy the momma chimp was slow getting well. But she very enjoyed the coddling. The other chimps lionized her over the event, even more than they did JC. After all, they had already come to expect heroism and cool moves, from JC. The baby was very proud of his mother. And never grew up to be a fagosexual. He became one of my best football players. Perhaps, he learned to tackle from his mother. ☺

When I asked JC where the Buckaroos were, for a few hours he only scribbled <I let them go>. He thought that was very funny. Hooting and chattering over it for over a week. I should never have let him watch that old Schwarzenegger movie, "Commando."

Soon I learned: The Buckaroos were living at Lancelot's cottage, home. Lancelot managed to take out a debt for their vet bills. Buck didn't heal so well. His age was now bringing him down. "The Lancelot House" became THE party spot, for the drug addict, snitch, and of course, pervert crowds.

(You can find "Cliff, on Fagosexuality", if you try hard enough. To the author's knowledge, it's still the most truthful, scientific and complete treatise on that subject.)

EVERYONE HAS THEIR PRICE

One evening, soon after my fourth NFL football game. I received a telephone call. "Hello?" "Is this Mr. Atreides?" "Yes. Who are you?" "That is not important." "Would you be Tom?" "Maybe." "As in Tom, Dick, Harry, and He's Hairy too?" My caller, Tom, just laughed. After a moment of silence, he continued "Certain very powerful people, have told friends of mine, that you have been associating with a certain, not quite sane, computer whiz, named Hiro. That is a very dangerous association, Mr. Atreides. I advise you to cease this association, beyond your play by mail games." "Thanks for the advice, but friends stand by friends. Hiro's more than a bit eccentric, but quite sane. I think he's got a winner. If the real nut cases don't have him whacked, that is." "Hiro claims to hear voices in his head, from people he never met, in lands far away." "Likely, that was just something he said, to weird out his fellow suits. When he put in his notice. He mentioned that they kept asking him the same questions. And weren't content with the same answers."

"Hiro attacked one of the assistant Cee Eee Ohs with a laser weapon." I had a giggle fit. (I must have caught it from Laverne.) "I would bet, it's no smarter to threaten Hiro in the real world, than to threaten him in a play by mail game. The way I heard it. … Hiro cut his tie neatly in two. And barely singed his shirt underneath. Then, Hiro, in a few seconds, turned his plastic coffee mug to slag, coffee boiling, steaming, and scorching the veepee's desk." "That's about what my source said." Tom admitted. "Say. I didn't think even you guys had anything good." "We do not! That is another sore point. He will not sell it to the government. Nor to anyone he thinks might sell it the government. He calls us a bunch of communist warmongers. … You are keeping some pretty rough company, Mr. Atreides." "Hiro told me, it would be very hard to market. A lot of fine tuning of crystals and capacitors, that he could teach only a few people. Not subject to mass production techniques."

"Even so, a few every few day could have a lot of subtle uses. Hell! Our best calls for an 80 pound backpack. And his runs off a motorcycle battery, and hits harder. … Do you think you could talk him into showing you how?" "Yes." "Great! I think I can get you ten million dollars, if you succeed –" "I didn't say I would do it, Mr. Tom. That would be betraying a friend. And now that I have so much money rolling in, I'm spending a lot of it, on a hair brained Moon Colony scheme." Tom was suddenly silent, surely in shock. I continued "Tell you what! I'll see what I can do. I'll explain it to Hiro the realpolitik realities. He can't have all 3, the Moon Colony, his laser, and his life. And if he discards his life, he can't have the other two. But you'll have to get someone to do something for Hiro and me. I want Hiro to have a one-page ad in U.S.A. Today.' And a small weekly ad, in the classifieds, at the standard price, as long as he wants, anytime he wants."

"You could buy that anytime you want. By yourself!" "No, not for Hiro. And not for a Moon Colony, any way. There are those who have frozen Hiro out on that, and all of the other top quality advertisement." Tom replied sarcastically, "I wonder who? Do you really think that will solve Hiro's problems?" "Maybe. If anyone can do it, Hiro can. In any case, the high profile should add a couple of years to Hiro's life span. That would, make Hiro very high profile." "Alright! Alright! I suppose it would be good if we had a real space program. And in a perfect world, Hiro should have his snowball in hell, chance of getting by all the sleaze. But it is going to cost. And I am not going to guarantee that both of you are nor going to die, real soon." "How much?!" "I do not know. I will get back to you. … Try to last a couple of more years yourself, if you can. I have already made enough on you, for a nice retirement.

But the more money, the merrier. ... You are a lot of fun Mr. Atreides." <he hung up>

Hiro's picture would be in the dictionary, next to "quixotic", if Don's wasn't there already. But he's no fool. I talked Hiro into selling the Laser. I had no problem, talking him into slow walking the project for a few years. (I wanted us chimps to have them first. Beat the hoomies in the light sabre race, sort of speak.) Hiro's "U.S.A. Today" ads cost me an even one million dollars. And nearly cost me two million, when I tried to negotiate.

Following is the highlights to Hiro's one page U.S.A. Today ad.

In big headlines "We need 300 Brave Adventurers to Leave Earth Behind, And Colonize the Moon!"

In simple large type: "One way ticket!" "Anyone who we consider space worthy enough can buy a ticket for $120,000,000. Others, who we consider top quality space workers, exceptional genes, or very good looking etc., can get a "ticket" for $60,000,000 or less. A few rare superpersons could get a ticket free." "Nothing on earth, can compare to jumping, running and walk-hopping, at moon gravity." "Build your own world!" "Jobs paying $40,000 an hour and more!" "Did you know, a bicycle on the moon, can be pedaled at over 200 m.p.h.?" Be one of the first 300 people on the moon, to claim real estate equal in size to Africa." "Solar panels on the moon, produce more than 100 times the electricity they do on earth." "Spread your genes thru out the galaxy!" "It's the human destiny, to populate the galaxy!" "Explore the new frontier." "$100 for an application." "$20 a year for our Newsletter." "All donations will be appreciated."

The money started rolling in for Hiro. But not near as much as we hoped. The powers-that-be, still had Hiro frozen out. Where Hiro solicited, they counter solicited, with max pressure. Hiro had a broad base following, of over 10,000 fanatics. Even though, they knew that less than 100 of them would ever make it to the moon. One hundred+ millionaires are a very closed clique. And even anyone with 10 million, dared not break ranks.

It was soon when I truly knew, that the hoomy species had lost its Space Faring Destiny. And would sink to constant barbarism. The major pestilence, on a very over populated planet. Turning all of the earth into a garbage heap and cesspool.

Then, in around a year, a glimmer of hope. But some might think, it was just more proof of the hoomies' spiraling downfall. ☺ A womens' lib fanatic lady inherited over 300 million dollars. Her name was Allison Rand. She financed Hiro with 250 million of it. But with some conditions.

The conditions: (1) It was negotiated that Allison and 5 of her female comrades, would be scheduled for 10th thru 15th colonist. That for 250 million was cheaper than all but Hiro's most optimistic "ticket" costs. (But still, 250 million had the program cash flush. Almost, to the point, of getting the first rocket there. Hiro saw no problem, with making up the difference with higher ticket prices, later.)

(2) The government would be elected by the sexes voting separately. And would be 5 councilpersons. 3 female, 2 male. (3) Although the fem Nazis wholly agreed we should have a scientific selective breeding program. They insisted that the men should be bred for strength, and little else. While the women would be breed for brains. And, that colonist should be selected for those traits.

Well (3) was mostly shot down before the money actually changed hands. Hiro, insisted on his own control of selection. And that breeding, would be mostly the choice of breeders. My own e-pamphlet declared that the colony would be a fanatic tool user society. Constantly constructing more and more. Calling for everyone to have a lot of brains. And, that strength's main measure, would be strength per body weight. And even to some degree, strength per food use. That pamphlet helped Hiro's cause, at least a little bit. It even mollified Allison to some small extent. She liked my suggestion that there should be a few more women, sent than men.

I also mentioned that child raising, a traditional female role, would be very important on the moon. We had a landmass the size of Africa to populate. And if the children were not a lot better raised than projects children, the Moon Colony would perish.

I also mentioned that women were a lot more important than men, because they did the main work of breeding. Anything else, was a nice bonus. But we couldn't send many excess women. Because if we treated them like a hen house, with just a few roosters, less worthy women would want to go to the Moon Colony. … That, caused a hissy fit among the fem Nazis. And a general uproar among the rest. (Lots of fun!) ☺ (1) Had already been hotly negotiated. But solid. (2) remained in place. But with one major modification. That the colonists could amend their constitution, with a 2/3rds majority vote. (I believed, that worked very well for my moon nationalist faction. Because such a crazy fem nazi constitution, would soon be amended. The first control of imperial earth, would be cut.)

IT'S NOT HOW YOU PLAY
THE GAME THAT COUNTS,
IT'S THE OWNER(S)' BOTTOM LINE

By this time. My chimp football and basketball teams played every two weeks, against NFL and NBA teams. Except after our first 3 games, the NFL refused to play us during regular seasons. We never got into the big money. But we did get $1,000,000 for every game we played. And another one million, if we won. We won about as many basketball games as we lost. And we never lost a football game. Until the rules changes.

The rules changes: The famous chimp play, is called the "chimp pass". "The Chimp Pass was outlawed." A chimp carrying the ball, hops onto the hands of 2 chimps, one chimp per foot. Those two, well practiced, heave him up and away, with all their strength. Literally, passing the chimp. After that, we started losing a few more basketball games. And we lost about 1 in 3 football games. … It wasn't such a big problem with basketball games. We usually lost the ball, when it failed. And often the projectile was hurt. With only 5 men on the field, basketball style coverage, it was hard to set up. Still, it was a big crowd pleaser. A slam dunk chimp pass, makes a regular slam dunk look tame. Especially when it fails!

But in football, it was a different thing. It was almost guarantee of a 5+ yard gain. Then the hoomies came up with the swat-the-chimp strategy. That strategy made our "3rd and one" conversions less than certain. But still very good. (Any decent football strategist can tell you, how often your offense makes a 3rd and one, is one of the strongest measures of how good your offense is. Especially if you are playing The Trogs or are The Trogs. [10]) When the hoomies were successful, it looked like a volley ball game, with the chimp for the ball. Occasionally, once or twice a game, one was 2 handed slapped by more than one hoomy. Sometimes for a big loss. The fans loved that!

Now that the money was rolling in. I spared nothing on my chimps. Vocational, trade, skills, to college courses. We pioneered in chimp specific medicine. Within a year, our own, were better than vets. Although I dared not let them loose on the Internet. I bought an Internet café. Transported and set it up, closed circuit, on the farm.

---

[10] I got that name from the scientific name for chimps. Trogyldite.

It's been a big debate whether chimps are physically tougher, that is, take hits better than hoomy pro football players. But no question that hoomies helmet butt harder. Chimps hit a lot harder pound per pound. But, hoomies have a very lot more pounds. With the rule change, the casualty rate went up from 3 to 1 hoomies favor, to 5 to1. Worse, the total losses nearly doubled. And chimp v. hoomy games were already a lot bloodier than hoomy v. hoomy. Our losses usually ran around a half dozen, and sometimes a dozen or more. We almost lost the first game after the new rules. Because by the middle of the 3rd quarter, when the hoomies were hammering us with their 2 power runners. I was down to low, and getting lower, quality replacements.

The hoomies complained that playing us wasn't a real football game. It was more, like basketball. One defense scored more than half as many points as our offence. But there was one big difference than basketball. We didn't have to dribble the (darned!) ball. We only lost the ball to a whistle, when one of us was slammed dunked into the ground. We could grab, tackle and pry the ball out of a hoomy's hands. Cool! Too bad we couldn't bite. It would be the hoomies that would have to quit, because they wouldn't have enough men on the field.

Our guys didn't weigh much more than the chimp average 110 pounds. You can be sure, that very embarrassed the NFL. ☺ Chimps bigger that 120 pounds, began to lose more of their fantastic strength per pound, with all the added weight. (Much the same, as you hoomies lost a lot of your strength per pound ratio. When your men bred your women for "curves". And your women bred your men for "hunks". Well, I and JC believe there is another reason(s) for that. But, I'll mention that much later on. By the way, wild chimps are trog.-trog., while JC breed chimps are trog.-superior.

We still had our high school games. Even football! And guess what?! We never won a high school game, after our first NBA game. Our fee was a nominal $500 a game. And another $500, if we had won one. We booked for months in advance, a game a week. Because my boyz played every week, I decided the needed a soft, relaxing, game every other week, odd weeks football, even weeks basketball. The opposite schedule of our NBA and NFL games. And beyond a bruise or three level of hurt, not a single kid was hurt by a chimp in any of those games, I did indulge in a wee bit of gentle corruption. Instead of our usually, lottery ticket style self-invitation offers. Every 3 or 4 games, I accepted a bribe. Sometimes very high! After all, it would take a lot more than my lifetime, to play every high school team in the U.S.A.

And yes, the University of Alabama was the only college team we ever played. Several times a year, when an NBA or NFL team wasn't available.

The chimp soldier training center never made as much money as I hoped. But before I broke into the NBA and NFL, $100,000 a year guarantee seemed fantastic. It did, give me the opportunity, licensing, and excuse to have all sorts of military hardware. Lots of fun! And it gave me a good cover, to militarize my JC chimps.

No JC chimps were part of my teams. And not even the JC gened rejects were made chimp soldiers. I was too cautious about risking some fed agent taking a blood sample from one of them.

I was rolling in money. Every month, I looked at my books, to see if I had a spare million I could donate to Hiro's Moon Colony. Most months, I sent a million. Although Hiro did not make his corp. a tax deductible charity. To better resist government etc. nosiness, and influence. I set up a non-profit tax deducible charity corporation, "friends of Hiro Society," so I and others' could get tax breaks. As Elmer Fudd used to say, "Dere's more dan won way to skin a wascally wabbit!" But alas, it seemed not to do much good. But what the heck, I needed some hopefully good thing to blow it on. Hiro kept joke assuring me, "million here and a million there, and pretty soon it starts adding up to some real money." But yes, there's a lot of difference between a million, and over a billion, that Hiro needed. And I knew I didn't have much time to make much difference.

Well, everyone starts leaving the party etc., when I start talking in much detail about chimp sports. So, I know you guys won't want to buy many pages of that. Still, I wouldn't be fully telling you the story, unless a I highlite at least one of the Trogs' games. ...

One of my favorite games ... well I don't think any of my favorite games are all that good an example. Here's one I remember pretty well, about a good an example as any. Our second game v. the San Francisco Raiders. (Yeah! Those guys just can't seem to make up their minds about where they want to live.) ☺ 3, maybe 4, games after the rules changes. They were wearing their pirate black. We were wearing our gray with silver glitter. Because we couldn't wear our black with multicolored glitter, while the Raiders were wearing their black. Yes, I and my chimps like glitter. And opposing fans love it, when hoomies knock patches of glitter off of our helmets and uniforms. But, we just glitter up again, during half time.

They got the coin toss, and so were receiving the ball. I still don't why hoomies think receiving the ball first, 1st half, is such a big thing. It doesn't matter to us. Kicking off isn't our forte. We very avoid it. Because we usually get hammered on kickoffs, we put in 7 second stringers for that. 2 mediocre first string defense players, the kicker, and Greg. Yes some well probably get hurt, so we minimize our losses, and put 7 expendables up front.

Remember Greg, from our first high school basketball game? Yes, that Greg. He's much better suited for football. He loves it. He's a multipurpose player. One of my best. So valuable, I only use him half of the defense plays. When it counts. He doesn't like that, and doesn't understand it much. But he knows that I'm smarter than him. Normally, he's a center safety. Short yardage, he's a linebacker. When it comes to busting a play, or making a big defense play, he's the man, er, the alpha chimp. I also use him on kickoffs. Which are pretty safe, for him. I put him deep center. To make slow motion hoomies waste time and motion, going left of right. Or else! Yes, he's too well known, not a surprise.

There's the kick! Steve did pretty good – this time. A fast line drive. By luck, it has a nice spin on it. The first hoomy center, should have tried to duck it. He tried to catch it, and did, after 3 seconds of fumbling it in his hands. Another few seconds, and it would have been a disaster. Unless, maybe, he fumbled it backwards. 5 of my chimps were almost on him. The other 2 second stringers were where they should be, covering left and right flanks, on the 50 yard line, just in case. The receiver did the best thing he could do, brought the ball, both arms, to his belly. And put his head down, thighs pumping like pistons, straight into the chimps. Yes, no one even thinks about carrying a football like a sack of bread v. Da Trogs. Stripping the ball is our forte. Superhuman. (He could have chose to fade back, and let his fellows try to form a line in front of him. But too late for any gain on that. He would have been just tackled a few yards back, instead of a few yards forward. 3 chimps met him head on. Whap! Whap! Whap! But he staggered on another yard. Then, the chimps had solid grips, stopping him in his tracks. And 2 more chimps grabbed him by a leg apiece, and threw him down. Then, as seldom happens in a kickoff, Greg got in on the action. Just as the hoomy was falling, Greg made a leaping but well aimed head butt, at a precise angle on the hoomy 's facemask. The facemask broke, the helmet flew off, and the hoomy went down, half unconscious. Seconds later, most of the Raiders slammed into the tackle. Pads popping, sounding like a dull machine gun burst. Raiders jerseys all on top of the tackle. But no fumble, because the receiver was still coddling the ball, in fetal position.

The announcer announced "Raiders have the ball, just inches from their forty five yard line, in good field position." What he didn't announce, was it wasn't the great field position that hoomies usually get. Greg hung around the field, while 10 more came in. A second string chimp had a cracked rib. He would not be back this game, unless we got more desperate for 11 players, than we ever had been. The hoomy receiver was the last off the field, glaring at Greg, who gave him the chimp chatter laugh. The hoomy was banged up a little, but would be ready to play, in a few minutes.

The Raiders threw a short pass, 11 yards. The receiver made another 3 yards out of it, but he paid for the 3 yards. It didn't look like he was hurt. But like chimps suffer from hoomies' helmets, elbows, and cleats. Hoomies suffer from chimps' superhuman grips. Hoomies have the passing game. Skilled, accurate and a big height advantage. Theoretically, short passes will get them 5+, more often 10+, yards all day long. But the reality is, throw too many of them, and hoomies lose the ball. Screaming chimps are usually seconds away from the quarterback, a finger on the ball can cause chaos. The ball might be grabbed from the receiver's hands. Or stripped after he catches it. … Long or middle range passes? Forget it! They're not even tried any more. No one can keep the chimps off the quarterback long enough. I replaced Greg for a few plays, or until something breaks.

Another smooth pass. Caught 5 yards further. But a chimp grabbed his ankle, and onto the Astroturf. with his other hand. But the hoomy, still drug the chimp another yard, while the chimp was making a groove in the astroturf. 2 more chimps grabbed him by the shoulders, and shoved his head into the astroturf. "Eight yards and maybe a foot. Second and just shy of 2 yards. " The receiver limped off the field, favoring the leg my chimp had gripped. That was nowhere near disabling. But he'd be carrying it, the rest of the game.

Coaching a chimp team is tense, but a lot of fun. Lots of strategy, but even more second guessing. Practically, any play can turn into a big play. I anticipated a run up the middle. Which should have been a surprise on second down. It would give their 2 of their 3 best receivers, time to recover a little. And should have been a very good chance of getting a first down. Instead of risking a 3rd down situation. 6 chimps rushing the quarterback. If it was a short pass, it would be very risky, both ways. 4 chimps in man to man coverage. And a flanking linebacker, being a chimp, almost means virtual safety. If they anticipated me, and did a play action, option quarterback run end around or pass; I'd be lucky if it didn't go all the way to a touch down. (Forget a simple end around. Hoomies just aren't that quick, nor fast, enough for that.) But, the biggest, dumbest, risk you can take, is not to second guess your opponent. (I "taught" the NFL that. Though, most insisted on learning the hard way. ☺)

As was, we both misguessed. I got luckier. My linebacker almost caught a panicked pass, batting it down. Although chimps are very poor at smashing thru NFL linemen, you cannot stop them for very long. Chimps will try to go over or under you. If you block too low, they might leap over you, with little delay. Too high, and that chimp might power his way thru you, and trip you besides. A lineman has to guess which the chimp will try. Because positioning himself "just right" is exactly wrong. Then, both chimp moves will work.

"Third and still under 2 yards." I sent in Greg. To stop a hoomy run up the middle, will call for at least 5 chimps rushing, to have a decent chance to hold it to any less than 3 yards. (And even then, it would probably be a ball strip, instead. A lot better.) That's what they "should" do. And what I "should" do. But what if they anticipated what I "should" do? Hmmmm. A short pass would be risky. A play action would be good. But not so good, as to generate a first down. And they weren't close enough for a field goal. Which has its problems anyway in a chimp game. Which leaves ... a screen pass. Considering the "shoulds", probably best to get the first down. And a pretty good chance of long yardage. Even perhaps all the way. So, I anticipated a screen pass.

I lined up 5 as if to rush. But only the one on the center did. (Never give the hoomies all the time they want!) The other 4 would go 2 apiece, to the flanks, as soon as the ball was snapped. Leaving Greg hanging back in center, watching, ready to make our play, or break their play. ...

It was a screen pass! To their right. The hoomie screen was penetrated before the ball was even caught. By the time the ball was caught, Greg made a bounding leap. He only touched a blocker, who was distracted elsewhere, with his foot, to kick off and at the receiver. Greg snatched the ball out of the receiver's hands. But the receiver still hung on, and held Greg's 110 pound self, and the ball, up in the air. Fortunately, the hoomies were mostly distracted, by the other chimps swarming in. But Greg took a head butt, and about a dozen weak elbow strikes, from unbalanced hoomies. In desperation, Greg shoved upward on the ball, breaking both his and the receiver's hold. And sent the ball slowly tumbling toward center field. Where Greg only guessed there would be a strong chimp presence. Greg was glad to fall down to the turf, and into a fetal ball. Away from those helmets, and all those elbows. For a second. Then, as the cluster fornication moved towards the ball, he was trampled by about a dozen cleats. One which "accidentally" stomped down, and twisted on part of Greg's back, that wasn't covered with plastic armor. Poor Greg! ...

As one of the chimp linemen went to the hoomies left, bound for the play, he was hit by the ball before he even saw it. But he managed to grab it. It he hadn't stood for a second or so in surprise, and then tried to run the wrong way, he might have gone all the way. 3 steps in the right direction, he was hammered by a hoomie helmet going over 20 m.p.h. That chimp was knocked down spinning, and the football fell loose as he was hit. (Even not carrying the ball, a chimp should watch all around for hoomies. Because "accidents" happen.) Fortunately, the other chimp that ran left, grabbed it. But surrounded by 5 hoomies, counting their quarterback, and no chimps he could see thru the walls of hoomy muscle. He wisely decided to just fall on the ball. The quarterback slapped him on the back with both hands, not at all gentle, "downing" him.

Da Trogs ball on our own 48 yard line! But that was a costly play. The lucky, then unlucky chimp was injured out for the rest of the game and several more games, too. But he did come back. (Thanks to our top quality, spare time, vets. And 2 mediocre doctors, besides.) Greg walked off the field erect, bleeding but proud. But for once, he was happy not to be in the game for a while. The vets finally cleared him, and he was back on the bench after half time.

Well, this is getting long, and I've only described 4 plays. So, I'd best just skip to the ending. But, you are getting the basics of chimp style football.

It was pretty low score for a chimp game. Both sides scored the usual lot of yardage. But back and forth. Most of the time, not passed the goal line. And the hoomies are very good at punting. Or course our punting sucks.

It wasn't looking good for the Da Trogs! The score, was 17 to 12, Raiders' favor. Raiders favor. Raiders had the ball on our 41 yard line. About 6 minutes left in the fourth quarter. Even if they scored a field goal, our chances would be extremely small.

The hoomies ran the ball up the middle, again. Running out the clock. They out guessed me, this time. 3 chimps tried and failed to get a hand on the ball carrier, while being pounded by 5 linemen. Greg was all there was between the goal line and the hoomy.

Greg was hit by a halfback, knocking him about 3 yards. But that was the ball carrier. Another collision. Greg managed to get one hand on the carrier's ankle. Not slowing the hoomy down all that much. But enough that he decided to stop, and use one hand to pry Greg's hand loose. A mistake. No single hoomie could pry loose any of my adult chimps' grips loose, by himself, even with both hands. By now, most of the chimps and hoomies surrounded Greg and the ball carrier, in one big violent huddle.

What Greg and the ball carrier managed to do, was tear the hoomy's pant leg off. Off the halfback went, for 3 more strides. Until Greg grabbed his ankle, yet again. The halfback had made first down, and going for more! The hoomy had to keep both hands on the ball, cradled next to his stomach, with both arms, too. Greg had him stopped cold. Then Greg got both hands on his ankle. Trying to jerk him off balance. But then, Greg noticed the halfback grimacing in pain.

Greg started to just grip and twist, and crush, on the ankle. Greg is very ruthless, and sometimes cruel. The hoomy's ankle wasn't tough enough, perhaps an old injury. He yelped and dropped the ball. He couldn't help but hopelessly grab at Greg's hands. But Greg reacted too quick for the (ex) carrier to even tough him. Greg had the ball and was squirming bull dogging out of the huddle. 3 hoomies made desperate lunging tackles at Greg. But one hit him so hard and solid, it looked like he'd be a pancake. But he walked away, with only a few bruises.

Alright! Chimps' ball. On our own 32 yard line. 5 minutes and maybe it was something like 30 seconds to go. Back in the ball game. But this was probably our last chance.

When the chimps have the ball, both sides look a little goofy. Very opposite of when hoomies have the ball. The only thing we're any good at, is end runs. Passing game? Yea, right. But it's a weak NFL team we'd be able to beat with just end runs. Once in every 4 or 5 plays, we have to do something different, to keep them honest. One of the things we do, is hand off the ball to the fullback, and let him wait for an opening. We often wait with the ball anyway, trying to wait until the sitz develops our way. And let the hoomies come to us, the better to avoid them. That does eat up the clock time. In fact the NFL came up with a special chimp game rule. If we (or the hoomies) take 2 minutes of clock time running the ball. The play is dead. 5 yard penalty from the line of scrimmage, down is done over. And only 2 minutes was lost. We don't have much problems with making first downs. Not unless we've lost 10 or more yards. Most often, by penalty. … Unfortunately, there wasn't enough time on the clock to push the 2 minute limit.

The hoomies field a lighter and quicker defense v. us. Except, there will invariably be 3 big bruisers on the field. They will always have 2 men on either side, already waiting for our end runs. The other 4, are their second guessing variables. Often, they will line up one way, and move different, when the ball is snapped. Or with a few seconds delay. Sometimes on short yardage, they send in a 4th or 5th big bruiser. In any case, as often as not, 5 hoomy linemen, hammer the poor 5 chimp linemen, who by rules, have to be on line. Part second guessing strategy, and part hoomy linemen choice, is whether they just hit for a few seconds, and try to eat the quarterback. Or keep on hammering the linechimp, hopefully out of the game. All of our linechimps are trained as centers. There is just too much turn over, to be specialized. We are pretty good at snapping the ball. We HAVE to be. And always to the quarterback, 5 yards back. Although every once in a while, the fullback takes his place. … What I'd give, to be allowed just one silverback gorilla!

The play begins. As usual, it was a good snap. As usual 5 hoomies rushing! Our courageous chimp line wasn't much more than a speed bump. But we very needed that critical second or so. This time, none of the hoomies spent much time hammering the line chimps into the turf. The linechimps staggered forward, 3 were a little dizzy, scattering in 5 directions, for about 5 yards. Waiting and recovering, to see what they could do to help. And yes, they were not eligible receivers.

The rushers didn't come close to Starbuck [11], our quarterback, so we had plenty of time. As almost always, he handed off. This time to our halfback, Fred. Fred didn't find any big openings. And the 5 rushers were still coming. So he ran for in between to hoomy, let's call them both cornerbacks. It was good for 5 yards. And he added 2 more to it, before he was grabbed by a linebacker, and he layed down on the ball (smart!).

---

[11] Actually, he was re-named after the great, old days, Dallas Cowboys quarterback. Not, the coffee shop. But Starbuck is easier to spell. I had to rename him. Goofy is not a good name for your best, sort of a star, quarterback. Starbuck is pretty good at passing for a chimp. Even better than most high school quarterbacks. Except of course he is pretty short.

With second down and 2 yards. And we very rarely did 2 non-end runs in a row. I decided another risky play. (Yes, what we'd just run was a "run left." It could have opted to an end run, but with no planned end run support from the other chimps. Us chimps aren't into that running thru a specific "hole." While the linechimps block the 2 opposing linemen aside.) ☺ I couldn't help being the risk taker that I am. Besides, us chimps NEVER punt on 4th down.

The play I chose was the chimp version of "The Long Bomb." Dreaded by both teams. Even though I might get lucky, I was really just crossing my fingers. Hoping that it didn't cause a turnover. But it should psych the hoomies, into keeping a man standing around in midfield. Funny how hoomies are always "closing the barn door after the cows run off." ☺ That would put one man less pressure on our end runs.

Our center snapped the ball, a little high. Which translated into a split second slower quarterback. Although 3 bruisers decided to punish our linechimps for about 10 seconds. Two other rushers kept coming for Starbuck. Starbuck barely got the pass off. The hoomies were so used to out quarterbacks running like scalded dogs, that they took a roughing the passer penalty. And Starbuck was a little goofy, the rest of the play. ... Starbuck never looked for a receiver. Nor did he even try to look over, or thru, that mountain of hoomy beefcake. He just tossed a high, slow, pass as far as he could, down the center field. The trick of the chimp version Long Bomb, is to throw the ball slow enough for the chimps to catch. But too fast for the hoomies to catch. Starbuck did a good, but not perfect job of that. ...

There was only one hoomy hanging around in center field. And he was only concerned with which way the end run was going to come. Or the off chance, that we'd try to run up the middle. Even so, he reacted well, and would have caught it. Except he collided with one of our wide receivers, who was "coincidentally" going for the ball, too. Leaving our other wide receiver, George, wide open to catch the pass. Although he had to stop to catch it, he built up some speed before the band of hoomies caught him. And he showed typical superior chimp breakaway speed. And lead the whole pack of hoomies and chimps by 10 yards, as he crossed the goal line. He was the only player on the field, chimp or human, that wasn't in the pile on tackle, in the Raider's end zone. Da Trogs 18! Raiders 17.

Joe our kicker, took the field for the extra point. Nice clean uniform. He gestured to the center and the ball holder, just to snap it directly to him. Joe caught the ball, and placed it carefully so he could grip it with his toes. Then, he threw it with his foot! Right thru the uprights! Of course, it was no good. It was throwing, not kicking. Even though Joe occasionally does manage to kick an extra point. I didn't blame him for showing off. An extra point. would not have made any difference. A field goal, and we lose. The crowd on both sides of the field laughed at it, and applauded. Which tends to translate into more tickets, concessions etc.

Yes there was still something like 3 minutes on the clock. But surely this is getting boring. So I'll just say; the Raiders didn't score again, and we almost did.

By the time the ess hit the fan, re: my sitz. Chimp teams ruined NBA Basketball and NFL Football. A lot like Mixed Martial Arts had ruined traditional pro boxing. Chimp v. Chimp teams might have pushed out most of the NBA and NFL. But I'd already cornered most of the chimp (slaves) market. So there were not many chimp teams. And by the time the other chimp teams started up. In Africa, any and all chimp sales were illegal. Although my chimp farm pulled chimps off of the endangered species list. The wild chimps, and their culture(s), were very endangered. And more and more. Even in Africa, over half of the chimps were domestic. That brought in, several breeding farms. And a lot of amateurs, who started out with a mated pair. (I slipped one nice old ma and pop couple, a pair of 1/8th JCs, that scored very high on the tests, as if they were half price rejects. Those 2, were trusted Cliff, and JC, loyalists.)

The one time I condescended to play another chimp team, football, I had to. They had beaten the Uganda national team. Time for me to put up, or shut up or lose a lot of money. The Silver Backs deserved a shot at us. But they only had a year of training and socialization etc. And frankly, out hoomy management was better, and smarter. Be careful what you wish for. In spite that we quickly started declining all but the craziest penalties, and played soft. And, after half time, I put in only second stringers. Except also Greg, who I already made promise me, to play nice, like it was a high school team. And we fiddled around enough, to score our only 2 field goals, ever. Even so, the score was 128 to zero.

Soon after that, came mixed hoomy and chimp teams. I ducked that, by telling the truth. The mixed teams have a big advantage over pure teams. I wouldn't subject my boyz to that. The truth I withheld, was that if we'd added hoomies ourselves. Those hoomies would get too close, and get suspicious about the strange goings on, at the chimp farm. Mixed teams take a lot of injuries. Especially the hoomies.

What really drove the NBA and NFL down to second class leagues, was the new "No" Rules teams. Everybody had finally come to their senses about referee and rules intense sports. I was always amazed, that the refs weren't the ones doing all the T.V. commercials. And whether you like this or not. Most hoomies do NOT want spectator sports LESS bloody than traditional boxing. They want more blood. Lots more blood! See the history of the Roman Circus Maximus.

Soon. Some evolved a lick or two of business sense. Diplomats were sent to neutral convention sites. And finally agreed to a standardized set of "No" rules, for each of the games. Surprisingly, they consulted me to pick the name for new-basketball, and new-football, teams.

Being the great diplomat that I am ☺, I choose names no league was using. Well. After I learned I couldn't get what I considered worthwhile bribes, for picking some League's name.

Football - - - > Bloodbowl. This came from a now obscure English wargame style board game. Touchdowns give 1 point. The first one to score 3 points wins. No silly passing rules. The play continues until someone scores a point. Or the rare penalty, that gives the victim a touchdown. Field goals are for vaginas, so no goal posts. The only Kickoff starts the game. And that's just the whistle blowing, so everyone can charge the ball, in the center of the field. There isn't surprisingly large volume(s) of rules. But almost all of that is over esoteric things, such as when knuckle and finger protection ceases to be armor (legal), and is classed as "nucks" (contraband). Armor is not uniform. And it varies a lot between players by style, tastes and "position". For instance, steel and Kevlar are as popular as high tech plastic.

Basketball - - - > Urban Brawl. Of ShadowRun roleplaying game fame. Played on Astroturf. A score is 1 point. No silly penalty shots. There are penalties, and in most stadiums intermissions, for the fans and concessions. But otherwise, it's one hour of continuous play. Dribbling is optional. But if you dribble, you can't be tackled nor punched. Armor is the old football type.

Women's traditional basketball is making a big comeback, in the N(ew)WBA league. But only because of that league's max height limit, scanty uniforms, and the prerequisites to make the team. That a player must place at least 3rd, in a regular, league sponsored, Internet voted, beauty contest.

Once the money was rolling in. I spent lavish amounts of money on my chimps. Several car and trucks, including two stick shifts, to play with, and practice on. And occasionally to "ride with" an adult hoomy. Vocational training videos etc. Deep stacks of books. I even bought an Internet café, and had it packed up and sent to the farm. I set it up closed circuit, farm chimps only. I couldn't trust to turn them loose on the Internet. But if ever they were emancipated, they would be as "computer literate" as any hoomy, of their brainpower. We pioneered chimp specific medicine. Soon, wisely, our sports chimps injuries, and treatments, were double checked by chimps.

If You Wish Your Kingdom Secure, Keep Your Moat Well Maintained

Soon after we finished the escape tunnel. I started work on a hide out. It was only for me, and few chimp retainers. Because unlike my chimps, I couldn't stay strong and happy forever, on fruits, roots etc. Nor could I run and hide near as well, from helicopters, planes, infantry divisions and tracking dogs.

I climbed the small fence in my backyard, officially in to chimp land. It was mostly trees, none much taller than 15 feet. It was once mostly planted pines. Now more desiccating, than rotting, stumps, were all that was left. I sold it "clear cut", to put pear, and pecan, trees planted in not very geometric rows. All sorts of less producing fruit and nut trees, for variety. An assortment of wild trees were still left from the pine tree days. The biggest were wild magnolias. That were doing very well, now that I'd cleared away scrub bush and pines. There were fig trees and very large blueberry bushes, growing in the shade of the other trees.

Nothing was in bloom. Only the pears and pecan were in season. The dominant smell was a musky, somewhat pleasant, scent of slowly rotting leaves.

A year ago, I had transplanted large saplings, just ready to produce fruit. And an assortment that young or older, from friends, who didn't give me much discount. In spite that, those were neglected, stunted by scrub brush etc. and dying. Left over, from the days of 40 acre farming.

There were an assortment of vines, more honeysuckle and wild grapes, than anything else. The grapes were gone wild French wine grapes. The grape skins weren't edible. So there was no market for them except for wine.

I passed a patch of dug up ground, where some chimps were doing a marginally successful garden. What the green shoots coming up were, I didn't bother to look close enough, to tell. JC's gardening instructions were already improving their little gardens. But the knowledge probably hadn't reached that plot's owners yet. I already picked up a distant following of mildly curious chimps. Most days, I didn't trek onto my land.

One of them hooted. That seemed to be a signal call. Perhaps they were already getting more organized. My path was clean. Except a few young ones, not "house broken" yet, my chimps buried their feces. Not only was it more sanitary and pleasant. It was building this rain leached sand soil, into rich orchard and cropland. A lesson hoomies should learn.

I walked around one of the 2 spring fed ponds, that my chimps used for water, and I occasionally fished. There was JC's hut. JC was already waiting with 4 other chimps. JC had a pick, 2 chimps had shovels. Another had a bucket, and another had a posthole digger. I was carrying a battery-powered drill, with a long wood boring bit, and an 8 foot "re-bar". (A narrow iron bar, frames made of them, were used to reinforced concrete.) One end of the re-bar sharpened to a nice point. A large ball peen hammer was stuck in my belt. We walked thru similar scenery, to the back fence.

More chimps added themselves to our parade. Then they disappeared, as we approached the fence. JC and his 4 helpers easily scampered over the fence. JC waited on the top for me. I had to take off my tennis shoes and socks. I put the socks in my pocket. And tied the tennis shoes together, and slung them around my neck. So that my toes could hold onto the chain link fence, and I could easily enough climb it. It was a big help to hand JC the re-bar, he tossed on the other side. His hand helping me up, was nice too. Once I'd straddled the barbed wire where no barbs were, it was easier climbing down.

I crunched down in the corn stalk stubble, and assorted mostly malicious and hostile weeds. To keep my head lower than of level with the brush. Because I didn't bother to ask permission to cross this farmland. Nor the farmer who owned the 40 acres beyond it. My chimps only needed their natural, knuckle dragging, stoop. With the briars and other varieties of thorns, and ankle grabbing creeper vines; this was far from a pleasant, comfortable, walk. But I was hardened to this stuff, from my youth. Thru the first 40 acre plot. Across a 3 strand barbwire fence, that I made with a handspring jump over. Thru yet another 40 acre plot. To a rise on a hump of land, that was too little to be called a hill. A lone 30 foot tall, but relatively squat oak tree, and some phillip grass, was all the vegetation there. By then, my socks were getting thread bear. I picked out the few thorns that had penetrated. Both ankles above my insteps, had scratches, and welts, puffing from green thorns' irritants.

I could hear the murmuring of a large moving stream. And smell the wet air. That I knew to be the Choctawhatchee River. (A small river. Some might call it a creek, during the summer dry season.)

The tree was convenient to my project. A little bigger, but less healthy than I remembered. Something, probably lighting, had split the tree near in two, growing in 2 upward directions, from a massive 6 or 7 foot trunk. I leaned the re-bar on the tree. Then I climbed up between the split trunks. It was hollow over a foot deep, in the main trunk. I started drilling with the long wood boring bit. I kept drilling small holes into others. Then I tapped with the head of my hammer to break chunks of wood loose. Then I removed them. 2 hours later, I had a wide, narrowing hole, so I could push the wood bore, with the drill, deep into the tree. Then I struck earth. Then, I pounded the re-bar into the dirt, with my hammer. Until the re-bar was flush with the wood. It had struck into a harder layer, an inch or so of dirt. That I guessed, as I hoped, was a shale, soft rock, layer.

Then, I climbed down the ledge, below the tree's hill. A few inches below the water, I knew was a shallow, level, shale bank. When the water would drop to reveal that mud slimed surface, someone with a rake could unearth broken stalagmites. I had regaled my high school science teacher, with about a half dozen of them. That was all that was left of a cave, that the river ruined, when its course changed eons, or at least centuries, ago. Except, I believed and was right, that there was one last compartment, inside the riverbank. Because of a small hole, that seemed like an animal burrow, but was not. And that exuded a very faint breeze of cool, cave like air, during the summer heat.

JC was returning out of that hole, widened by my chimps, but to just chimp size. He told me that there was indeed, a cave chamber, the size of a small living room. And his crew was expanding it, towards the tree, and the rebar. I left for my house. We decided that JC needed to accompany the chimps back home, to keep them out of trouble.

It was just the beginning, but it was an auspicious beginning. I wished I had tested my belief, when I was still a youth.

This was soon to be, our emergency hide out. Originally, we decided to disguise our entrance, and widen it for me. But with the inflow of big money, we just closed it up, after constructing, provisioning and furnishing. We dug a tunnel, so that its one entrance was underwater, at least 1 meter deep, even in the lowest known level ever, of that river. We had a well hidden, water proof, vermin proof, buried cache, of inflatable rafts, dive tanks and regulators, and dried fruit; 50 or so meters up stream. ...

Later. As I climbed over, the 3 strand barbed wire fence, into what a townie would call his back yard. I saw Laverne sitting on my back porch, giving sign lessons to a 100 or so collection of chimps. Not easy! But we'd long since progressed to where they teach each other. A true humanesque culture. (They 'd even be putting stones on sticks, and making fires, if I didn't discourage that sort of thing.) All she had to do, was teach several of the chimps, that she kept up front. And by next session, the rest would more or less know the lessons, too. And quite a few, that played hooky, besides. (She had a key to my backyard padlock.)

This was one of her unscheduled appearances. Usually that means, she would miss one of her coming scheduled appearances. She didn't notice me coming, until the chimps stood up, in what would pass for "Attention!" for them. (They are somewhat bipedal challenged.) And they put their right fists over there hearts. Then, their right hands opened, and dropped to their ankles. (Still standing straight.) An ancient style salute. (That JC! We were going to have to talk, about a more cautious Laverne – policy. I'd been thinking about firing her, and getting someone a lot less smart. But, well, I didn't have it in me. Besides, she still had a lot of use. Sometimes JC is worse than a hoomie teenager. Which in most ways, he pretty much is.) I gave them a return, same, salute, in my best imitation of a Brit field marshal. "Carry on!!!"

Laverne giggled and said "So that's how you do it!" I signed for them to sit down. But they were still stiff. <Giggle! Giggle!> So, I had to shake one of them, to loosen him up. And I forgot all my sign language, getting the others to loosen up. <Giggle!> "That's the roman civilian salute. I decided to teach it to some of the guys and gals." (By now she had me giggling too. So consider the rest of these " "s to be punctuated with 1 to 3 giggles.) "I want to see your notes!" "Err, ah, well, I didn't take any notes!" I tried to teach a few of them, but it didn't seem like I was making any progress. I think, they just stated networking together, at their best, like you said they would." "But I didn't think it would be this sudden! It should have been a gradual change. Anyway, be sure to always take notes. And probably because you've been socializing with the chimps more." (Yea right. <Author giggles> socializing, like in taking them to work details. Well, I got JC to help me with "my" notes.) "Well! Let's take advantage of this." I said, "I was wanting to teach a few of these guys, so they could teach it to my soldier chimps, across the road. How about, after this session, you take them over to my military chimps, and do your magic? I think my mil reps will be impressed with it." "Yes. The mil reps want me to see them at 6 o'clock, anyway. So, I'm going to have to take off Saturday, to study for my finals." She suddenly became frowny faced, and very not-giggly. Which caused me to blink out of giggle mode, too. She said "But we need to talk. They pay me by the month, not by the hour. Too many hours. My school is more important." "But we're in an opportunity-crisis here, Laverne. You've about done with this quarter. When you're thru, how about skipping a quarter, and helping me out?" She was still frowny, I continued "How much per hour would you be willing to work for?" She un-frowned, but not quite smiley, and far from giggly. She said blandly "twenty dollars." "And you'd be willing to skip a quarter?" She nodded. I could tell by her tones, that was a negotiating offer. Even so, I counter offered, as I was writing a check "One hundred dollars, my final offer. If not. Clear out your desk!, and out the gate!, by sunset!" We both started giggling again. I handed her the check, $10,000 for "$100 p.h. contract labor," "Let me know when you've worked thru that check." "Is there a trailer, or a cabin, or something I can rent close to here?! I want to put in a lot of hours! ... But let's get on with the lessons. You too." I pulled up an old kitchen chair, that I'd demoted to a lawn chair. I'd neglected my lessons so much, that I was NOT her best student.

EXPANSION, AND EXPANSION AND MORE EXPANSION!

That's a paraphrase of on my hero, and role model's, Danton. Although I had very tried to avoid Danton's concept of "Audacity, …", the chimp "revolution" had been very successful.

It was 16 years later. And I would have to finally do something audacious.

I now had over 1,000 JC descendant chimps. And most were at least 1/8th JC. Octoons, as I called them. As long as we used non-JC females with JC. I figured we could avoid the worst of the inbreeding problems, and still breed ¼, quadroons, together.

With our football team, basketball team, and my 20 acres across the "bridge," now being used for soldier chimps. And my non-JC breeder females, totaling another 400 non-JC chimps. My 40 acres was way too crowded. And I couldn't buy new land, and expand, without too. risking my already too risked security.

We did cull a lot of 1/8th or less breeds. Those that scored significantly higher that normal chimps, on our intelligence, and assorted aptitude, tests; we kept. Those that were not outstanding, we sold. Unless they were promising basketball or football players. What I ended up with, were far from JC clones. In fact, only around a hundred could fully socialize with JC. Those, were the leaders. We had a caste system, a lot like the folks in the projects. The reasonably smart led the not so smart, who led the dumb, who led the even dumber. But. I estimated another 15 years, and we would average equal to human intelligence. And then, because we selectively breed, and faster; we would surpass the hoomies.

So, we made a bold move. 800 of my JC chimps divided into groups of 50 to 100. And traveled stealthily at night, to areas with low hoomy population, wilderness, warm and with good food sources. 200 went to California. Those, I arranged to be sent in containers, by an 18 wheeler truck. With all the truck farms, and orchards, in California, nobody would notice what my chimps would pilfer. Those contained half of my elite chimps. Because they were in need of at least that much leadership. But I kept most of my best genes, still at my farm, to breed.

"If You Slay JCus, Then You Must Slay The Son's of JCus."

12 days after our chimp "colonists" left. May 5:03 a.m. Of what was to be a 5:47 sunrise. My computer emitted a loud, continuous, series of beeps, thru a speaker. For sure, an emergency. Most likely – we were under attack! I powered the computer on, which was programmed to auto turn the alarm off. In coming message from JC. <An outpost chimp heard unusual sounds, on our hearing devices. Then got an infrared visual on 3 chimps. We sent scouts. Those chimps are not our. Not Buckaroos. Obviously, the military underestimated us, and sent in chimp scouts, first. Let's go! I'm sending 20 chimps to carry your stuff. Don't carry too much, you'll slow us down. JC. Out.>

The chimps were there, before I finished dressing. I pointed to a few things for them to take, as I put my shirt, and light jacket on. Then I made a lot of hard decisions about what to take. I had my pocket pistol. But I entrusted the chimps with my gun collection and ammo. I pointed out several items in my lab, including a hand crank grinding machine. I ripped open some floorboards. And pocketed the one item there, a diabetic sized hypodermic needle, with its point stuck into a small cork. And wrapped with clear tape. I didn't trust them with my tote bag full of money. (Us hoomies are strange that way. ☺) I gave them 6 cell phones, that belonged to fictional people, and could do email [12]. We had more in the Hide Out, and they already had others. (The chimp colonists left with 2 per group.) …

All of the chimps were armed with roman style shortswords, and AK-7s, that had bipods screwed on, to enable our (light weight) chimps to shoot a lot better. They were chattering anxiously. Although they seemed to be more having fun, than scared.

Into the tunnel. Although there were 30 chimps left. Mostly young, and babies, I went first. I was a potential liability. The faster I got away. The faster we got away. Even though 4 feet wide, a 2 foot high tunnel is hard to crawl thru. And I had 50 yards to belly crawl. Small, very dim, 2 watt bulbs, illuminated the tunnel. Giving it a spooky glow. The hard packed dirt floor, gave off a musty, well,

---

[12]   Only about half of the JC chimps could do even the simplest e-mail. And we were gambling that the military would not realize that our chimps could do that. It would be less than not useful, if they found out. But one must take risks in war.

tunnel smell. A few meters into it, and I was grimy. All the other chimps ahead of me, were so far ahead, that I couldn't see them. Around half way, a chimp was waiting for me. He pointed to something beside him, and signed <dead>. Then, he scurried away.

When I got there I saw the snake. A little over 5 feet long, diamondback rattler. And it was not dead. Its back was broken. – probably my chimp fangs! By the looks of the gashes on it. Between its upper half, and still spastically twitching, and slapping, tail; it could very slowly creep. I've seen a lot bigger diamondbacks. But contrary to what Texans will tell you, a 5 foot diamondback is big. In fact, bigger than most Texans' 10 footers. ☺ It had managed to crawl to about center of the tunnel. And was now crawling about 2 inches a minute, towards me.

I took off a tennis shoe, and slowly pushed it towards the snake. The snake sunk its fang into the shoe toe. I grabbed it by the neck, with my other hand. (Normally, that would have been quite a handful, to hold on to. But its not–paralyzed muscles, weren't very strong.) I placed it on the far side. (I knew it would take hours to strangle the snake. And it was too big, to pinch, or twist, its head off.) I slowly crawled by, jammed to the right side, as I could manage. Extreme paranoid fear, that the snake would move faster than possible, and strike me. By the time I was looking back, it and a baby chimp were hissing at each other. A youngster was looking over the baby's head. I signed to him <kill>. Not waiting to see if he knew my sign, I kept going at my relatively, slow motion speed. I heard later, that he did kill it.

When I exited the tunnel, the sun had yet to rise. Lucky! There was enough starlight for me, to dimly see about 30 meters. All around, well hidden, were chimps with AK-47s resting on their bipods, pointing back the way we came. I think, about 20 on each side of the tunnel. I could dimly make out my 30 foot fence, because some of the metal glittered slightly, in the starlight. I could very dimly make out 4 soldiers, or at least humanoid shapes, which seemed like they were pointing their barrels thru my fence. About 10 meters apart. Obviously, my whole farm was similarly surrounded. Because some sound, likely my own, might cause them to look around. And the brush wasn't very high here. I had to belly crawl some more, now thru briar, sticker grass, and who knows what else.

The rest of the chimps came out of the tunnel, and could more pretty quick, and still be concealed. With sort of a high crawl, that dangly chimp arms, makes them very good at. Then the little guys that were protecting us with the AK-47s, passed me too. Except for two, who were detailed to stay last, and protect me. About 10 meters beyond, I could high crawl. Another 20 or so meters, and I could often stand. But at night, even that made this trip thru the brush, an ordeal by thorns, vines and sharp twigs. Once past the first 40 acres, it was better, but still horrible. Because it was planted corn, about 4 foot high. But even here, some man-eating weeds had grown up among the corn.

Not much later. I exited the tunnel. The first faint glow of the sun appeared, as it was about to rise in the east. Seconds later, thousands of guns went off, some of them firing in bursts. None of that had a distinct sound, like a continuous rumbling thunder, as if from a greater distance. I could smell the burnt powder, drifting towards us in the wind. "Cordite", as the military novelists oft describes the smell.

Shortly into the corn patch, we made a wide semi-circle loop to our right, then, about 100 meters down, we looped back again to the same straight path, to the rafts etc. cache. I heard a few coughs, and one murmur sounding conversation, too far off, for me to make out any words. And it was still half dark enough, that I saw several cigarette glows. So I knew that we're circling around some military units, in reserve. ...

The cache was picked clean. Waiting, roped to a bush at the water's edge, was the last raft. All it contained were 4 chimps, and their AK-47s, and 5 dive tanks, with regulators attached. We were quickly to the cave entrance, with only a few strokes of the oars, just to guide. There, was a problem.

This was pretty high water, but not unusual in the spring, with heavy rains. The water level was about 6 meters above the entrance hole. Waiting, anchored to rocks on the bank, were 6 rafts, crowded with 43 more chimps. (The original plan, called for only 8 chimps, JC and me. Hence only 10 dive tanks. Well actually, just the regulator limit. We had 10 more tanks, inside the hide out. In spite that the plan had changed to 40 chimps, counting JC. We never got around to adding more tanks and regulators. We decided we'd need lots of messengers, on hand ready. But that's only a small problem. …

Chimps are phobic about water, especially diving under it. I had accustomed mine, to recreational swimming. And outdoor bathing. But this was more than a little too much. Of course, "everyone knows" that hoomies swim like fish. So, they used the courage given to the better sort of humans, and chimps to overcome their phobic fear. Well, at least to wait patiently here, for me to heroically lead them. But this hoomy had been eaten alive, by briars and the like. Frankly, the water looked very scary to me, too. I'm talking fast, turbulent, dirty sewer looking brown. (Just tree leaf "tea" and clay, but still.) And completely opaque. And pretty cold, too, for a southern guy. Still, I steeled myself to do this thing, for the greater glory of chimpdom. And I got even more "courage" from the terror of hoomy hordes, that would soon come to massacre us.

The always resourceful JC already had a gigantically long rope, made of at least four 10 foot long ropes knotted together. This was noosed around my chest, just under my armpits. The idea, I would swim to the entrance. Then pull the rope, so they'd know to follow, handling the rope. ... I splashed into the water. Down I swam, helped by the extra weight of the dive tank. I found the ledge, where the stalagmites were. Holding against the current, that I couldn't come close to swimming against. I managed to find the drop off. Then, being drug along. I felt further below with one hand, to find the entrance. Not really all that dangerous. Unless the VERY unlikely event, that there was a big, hungry, alligator, waiting there for me. Not a pleasant thought! But soon, I realized that I'd gone too far, or missed the hole.

I swam up, and waved one of my arms above the water. They caught on, and hauled me aboard one of the rafts. With my new knowledge of about where the drop-off from the shelf was. I realized I'd started down stream from the entrance. We tried again, well above where the hole should be, so I'd be sure not to drift by it, before I could search. This time, I was lucky. Not only did I find it, but I managed to drag myself inside. I made it up into the, only a little wet, And I was out of rope. And it was totally dark. I was unable to see a place to tie the rope, if there was one.

If I let it go, it would be quickly gone. Nothing to do, but go back into the water.

Near the exit, I tugged again. I could tell by the tugging, that I'd tugged a chimp out of the raft, but he was still hanging on. Well, that would work. I crawled back up towards the room, hoping that they would not tug me, nor the rope out of the entrance. And we'd have to start all over again. ... To avoid writing the boring, I'll just say we made it.

As soon as I had a chimp to hold the rope. I scrambled around until I found the light switch. Then I turned on the small electric heater. As an after thought, I turned on the ventilator blower. We had plenty of electricity. At least, for a long while. 12 luggage trunk sized batteries. That I understood were designed to power forklifts.

Then after about a half hour of picking out thorns, splinters etc., and salving my many scratches, deep and shallow. And after making and drinking a hot bowl of soup. I wrapped myself in one more blanket than I'd normally want, and immediately went into a deep sleep, until around noon.

The 7 with the rafts, did their best to hook up with the others. Who broke down into 50 to 100 chimp groups. A lot like the earlier "colonists" chimps, but much better armed.

The plan, was to lay low for 30 days. Each colony, original and new refugees, would send one message to the Internet chat room, that we had in common. We in the Hide Out, would only log on, to "listen", not answer, to others' news and problems. But no one liked hiding out in a gloomy cave for 30 days. The chimps had a marathon conference and debate, about what to do. When I woke up, at first I only watched the signs, and the typing on the computer screen, I was busy brewing and drinking tea. And preparing myself a "feast", of dried fruit and beef jerky. Their discussion went nowhere. JC was the most pessimistic. He knew better than any of us, the folly of fighting the U.S. military, in anything like a conventional warfare style. …

I fingered my clear taped hypodermic needle and thought for a while. "The die had been cast", as Julius Caesar would have said, since the day I and JC had become comrades, I laid the hypo needle on the kitchen table sized conference table. And said "I got it from an infected boil of an infected steer. Long ago. But is has a long shelf life." That was an item I'd acquired long ago, when I was a revolutionary. I continued "The only good way to destroy a superpower, is with a superpower weapon." JC tapped on the computer screen <Destroy?!?> "Anthrax." <Not much!> "We'll use it to make as much as we need. After, we wait 30 days, for the searches to slow down. I propose the gentlest possible use, and still smash the government. Simply force 50 of the largest cities to evacuate. A wrecked economy, and nearly half the people homeless and jobless." <Lots will die fighting over food etc.> "Can't be helped. It's us or them."

The government raid on my chimp farm, was not entirely a no casualty farce. The first wave of shooting, was at everything on my farm that might conceal a chimp. My house nearly collapsed, from so many bullet holes, in supporting timbers! Except the 20 acres across the street. They sent in 4 warrant officers, special animal handlers, who had worked with soldier chimps. Thru 4 different holes in the fence. That had already been cut. With wire cutters. (Triggering our silent alarm. ☺) After all, they wanted to collect this valuable collection of our half trained military weapons.

When JC was first aware that there were strange chimps inside our fence, he sent a JC breed chimp as a messenger. There was a normal chimp, who was never sold, there. He just helped train chimps. And he was very loyal to us. He kept, not very alert, guard at night. Secret to all but several chimps, who were never sold, we had a buried weapons cache, in the center of their huts.

As hoomie handlers crossed into our side of the fence. The 200 soldier chimps open fired with civilian version M-16s. The 4 chimp handlers were turned into hamburger.

But most of the bullet barrage was directed at where they knew, or suspected, other hoomie soldiers to be. In less than a minute, the chimps had killed or wounded more than their number. The hoomies fled in panic. Losing more than a few more. The reserve units and officers, managed to pull back together, a thin picket line, 300 meters or so away from the farm.

If the chimps had charged, or even if someone snuck up on one, and yelled "Boo!", the hoomies would have routed again.

The smart thing to do, would have been to charge thru the hoomies. Then run and hide. And keep running and hiding. But the JC breed chimp was chosen more for expendability, then brains or military strategy and tactics. What he did do, was inspire, and order his troops, and fight like a tragedy bent Viking.

In about 15 minutes, the other hoomies gathered up, as many as they thought they could spare. Which wasn't so many. About 400 hoomies, with some heavy weapons, such as belt loading M-60 machine guns. The confusion of my deserted chimp farm, had them sending all kinds of troops chasing "ghosts". And they counter attacked the chimp soldiers. The attack turned out to be a thick ranked frontal assault. (Everyone was following orders.) A lot of chimps were killed. But they were not really in touch with the reality of modern killing machines. They always took this soldier stuff as a game. They didn't have the good sense to rout. No hoomies could have done as well. It might have been the chimps RPG-9 round[13] that routed the hoomies. 4 more, blasted into thick groups of hoomies as they ran. It was long after daylight, before anyone who had fought the chimps, mustered the courage to fight again.

Once there was full daylight, the military very completely established order and discipline. Most, including 8 attack helicopters, pursued the retreating chimps. Who fortunately, had many kilometers head start, in back water river swamps. And then into deep forests and planted pines.

But 3 infantry companies attacked from 3 sides. The road was held by an infantry platoon, with 2 more (total of 4) belt loading M-60 machine guns. To make sure none escaped. And all nine 81 millimeter mortars. Firing from Lancelot's front yard. The mortars could not both fire, and keep up with the chimp hunter teams, chasing chimps in almost jungle terrain. So they stayed there.

It was an anticlimax. By the time all the chimps with ammo shared with those without, they had less than 3

---

[13] Rocket Propelled Grenade launcher. A modern, updated, version of the bazooka. Ours, were Pakistani copies of the Russian model. (All weapons are cheaper and better in Pakistan.) We had 9 more with the retreating chimps. But we only had 40 RPGrenades. We also had, with the retreat, 10 M-60 machine guns.

rounds apiece. Including bullets that had already been scrounged from the dead. … By the time 27 mortar shells hammered 20 acres. With a long series of ear splitting <Whump!>s. There was little there that wasn't totaled, much literally blown to pieces. And flying shrapnel pieces, at that. There would not have been many chimps left alive there either. If they hadn't already dug foxholes, well chimp holes. ☺ Those blasts were quickly followed by a non-stop bullet barrage. That deadly and hellish combination suddenly brought my chimps in complete, graphic, touch with battlefield reality. In fact, only one of them wouldn't have surrendered then and there. If they'd been given a chance. The hoomies one-helicopter gunship cruised along; firing its paired guns. Churning up a nasty dust storm, that advanced into the chimps. It methodically turned several chimps into chimp burger. And would have slain quite a few more, before running out of ammo. And going back to reload. But a chimp managed to heroically fire the last RP grenade at it. But, undoubtedly because of his shaking hands, he missed an easy shot. Even so, the 'copter might have set a speed record for a climbing U-turn. After all, he didn't know we were out of ammo, or if we had more rocket launchers. So he left the chimps alone.

The JC breed chimp was probably the only chimp there, to fight a hoomy in close quarter combat. After emptying his M-16, and one he snatched from another chimp, who was trembling, curled up into a fetal ball. He chopped the hoomy's neck in two, with his roman style short sword. Seconds after the hoomy shot him 3 times. Bullet wounds he would die from, in a very few minutes.

There were 43 chimp survivors, most of who had bullet(s) in them. They had been raised as soldiers, from birth. They were now irrevocably traumatized. They were no longer any use, not even as chimp soldiers.

We didn't hear this from any of the local papers. Although they had the stories too. There was nothing about it on the Electronic Brain Sucker (TV.). We heard it from very round about Internet sources. Within an hour of the attack on my chimp farm: 10 fed swat team looking folks, drove up in a van, at Lancelot's cottage house. They shot the Buckaroos to pieces, with full automatic fire. Israeli made Uzis. And they drug Lancelot, crying over his dead chimps, hands cuffed behind his back, and into the van.

No one seems to know what happened to Lancelot. Perhaps, some of their help setting up the attack on my chimp farm, was bad info. I never tried very hard to find out, why. But many years later, Tom said he was told, they knew too much, and would have been an embarrassment. Sort of funny, Lancelot disappearing, or worse, because he knew too MUCH.

The retreating chimps faired better, 8 of the slower, and dumber, non-JC baby chimps, were their only losses. (Yes, the vile hoomies didn't follow any conventions of war. They murdered adults, females and children.) Many of the chimps considered it a fun game. After the 3rd helicopter gunship was destroyed by RPGs, the hoomies stopped using helicopters. Then, when chimps manning 2 M-60 machine guns, backed with 20 rifle chimps, shot up a large dog, and dog handler, team: aggressive pursuit was called off.

Much later. I learned how they became very suspicious that JC was with me. Their weekly infrared aerial photos, showed a lot less chimps, than there was, a week before. Although Laverne didn't know anything, and was loyal to me. Once that sudden extreme paranoia kicked in. they looked into the college records, on the secret sly. Of course, her reports triggered all kinds of warning alarms. In fact, her results and observations were so different from the norm, that she was getting famous, among any scientists, of any science, that had much relation to chimps. They had already been collecting info of my buying and selling. Now, they seriously studied them. The data was very consistent with doing exactly what I was doing. That is, running the farm, primarily to breed JC chimps. Extreme paranoia escalated into out right terror. They were not completely sure. But rather than do further investigation, and risk me knowing they knew – they struck!

2 days later. Our sound pickups, in the tree above our Hide Out, transmitted assorted dog sounds. Mostly, barking and braying. Soon, our screen watcher chimp saw, and showed me: It looked to be about 10 rifle soldiers, with 3 civilian dog handlers. 4 doberman and 8 (obviously deer hunter) beagles.

Some of the dogs were sniffing the air. And they mostly sniffed in our direction. They were meandering in our general direction. I instantly guessed! I turned off our feeble air circulating blower. Which was blowing out of a small pipe, that was blowing out near the top of the tree, that was above our Hide Out. I signed, and whispered "Shhhh!". Chimps even woke several up, and signed them to be quiet. There were a lot of sign conversations, that I saw little of.

Soon, the dogs, handlers and troops were hanging out around our tree. A doberman climbed the tree, growling, as far as he could manage. But he became confused and frustrated, and he slid back down the tree. After awhile. The dogs stopped whining at the tree. But they still looked at it, intently.

It was a VERY scary time! If a hoomy climbed that tree, he would have near certain seen our tiny speakers and lenses.

The hoomies sat down, unconcerned, for a smoke break. And they hoomy-chattered together. Among the things they picked up, "Probably a coon was here last night." They could see from the ground, that there was no chimp in that tree. They left in about 10 minutes. But we were all nervous until the sunset. Then, I switched the vent blower back on. Our air was still plenty breathable. It was now very musty. But it was always a little musty, anyway, with that feeble blower. And I was conditioned to it, by then. After that, I was never completely comfortable in the Hide Out.

FORTUNE FAVORS THE BRAVE!

Something like a month before the feds raided my chimp farm. Hiro, my moon colony, gamer, e-friend: was still not doing well, with the moon colony project. Although he had accomplished a lot, in research. And had a few good prototypes of needed special equipment and such. And arranged for relatively cheap production of large numbers. Most notably. photoelectric cells designed specifically for moon's sunlight. And a neat device, that turned CO_2 into O_2 + C in the form of powdered graphite. At the cost of a lot of electrical power, that could be easily supplied by superior moon based solar energy. And extremely air tight door seals. And powerful, but light and compact, very durable, gas pumping and bottling gear. Yet, Hiro was at a point, where he was "spinning his wheels".

Until, Enter Chuck the Barbarian. Famed play-by-mail gamer, most notably of Super Nova <u>IV</u>. Otherwise, a rich kid bohemian, not quite ne'er-do-well. One can't blame him for leading aimless, leisurely life, of a wandering low budget perpetual tourist. Especially as his super-rich father cut him off, from all financial, or influence, support. For some real or false, indiscretion, heinous offence, or whatever. I never found out what. It would seem, the scandal sheets would have dug up whatever it was. So me thinks, Hiro must have done some computer wizardry, to erase whatever it might be, before Chuck became famous. After all we prefer our heroes untarnished. And we especially can't blame him, because he became, arguably, the greatest hero of our century.

In spite of whatever, Chuck got over 90% of his father's inheritance. Which after taxes, fees, extortion etc. came to a little over 268 million. Without seeming to spend much thought on the idea, Chuck gave Hiro 250 million. On 3 conditions. The biggest was (1) Chuck would be the first moon colonist on the moon. (2) Chuck would be, at least the 5th highest ranking person in the colony. (3) The next flight after his, would contain Chuck's new wife, chosen in sort of a beauty, athletic, and brain power etc. contest, that Chuck would finance himself.

Hiro had a lot of misgivings. (1) He was a little short, soft, and muffin looking. Chuck was far from what Hiro would have chosen to fly the first spaceship, and set up the first "camp". No one really knew whether Chuck was responsible and dependable. It was just that he never had any responsibility. He didn't have any of the skills, that a workman would have. He had attended a large assortment, of mostly low value college courses. Either to pick up on college women, or to learn something to do with whatever his current, low, or no, risk adventure, lark or hobby was. Nothing close to amounting to any sort of degree. Most of the courses that he actually did complete, had mediocre or less grades. He was well above average intelligence. But again, he did nothing with it, to gain even average wisdom, nor useful knowledge.

One thing he had going for himself, for the moon colony. For some reason long ago, he joined the Marine Corps. And for some reason, he stuck with it for 3 years. From them, he learned the discipline, that he finally, in his mid 30s, decided to apply. Within hours after the handshake on the deal, he fanatically drove himself to learn everything there was to know, about being a moon colonist. While he drove himself, Marine Corps style, to intense physical fitness. In a little over 2 months, when he made the flight, he was a brand new man. With a great purpose! But still LOOKED like a pudgy wimp. 2 months was not long enough, to gain intense physical fitness, and lose weight, both.

But Hiro shrugged his shoulders at Chuck's disqualifications. Around 50 million was what Hiro needed, to launch the first colony rocket. All Hiro had, and all Hiro did, was mostly just something like 80 million apiece. Chuck's money would cover 2 more launches, and a lot of change. Even if Chuck crashed and burned, Hiro would still be way ahead.

Before the first part of other rocket ship was tack welded to the second. Moon "tickets were offered for 45 million, to the very qualified. Softly scheduled starting 3 months, after the first launch. But Hiro knew he'd be selling some 90+ million dollar tickets to colonist of lesser value.

(2) 5th ranking colonist?! Hiro didn't like that much. And he had negotiated Chuck down from first rank, "Mayor" as Chuck called it. Hiro had more that his fill of corrupt, plutocratic corporate leadership. Between this decadent, spoiled, over aged, rich kid. And with Allison. Politics on the moon was way too "interesting". It did make Hiro less worried about Chuck "crashing and burning". ☺ (By the time the launch was near, Hiro gradually became somewhat impressed, with Chuck's newfound leadership potential and hyper responsibility.)

(3) Chuck's custom fit, beauty contestant, bride. Not a problem. With the right spin, a strong capable woman, for weak Chuck; Allison and the girls, would even like it. Ironically, she would be the first superior person, like which Hiro had been hoping that half of the moon's population would be.

With Chuck's liquidatable assets, and Hiro's ready-made plans and connections. It did not take very long to cobble together the first Rocket launch. Chuck merely bought out the majority shares of all the companies Hiro needed to do business with. And set them up with the big, but negotiated to not outrageously profitable, contracts. A good long term investment, any way. And he could always trade their common stock back later, instead of paying cash for things. ...

About 6 days before my chimp farm was raided. Chuck blasted off. The rocket was simpler, and a lot less expensive, than the original moon explorers' rocket. Nothing fancy, nor any hair brained ideas to re-use anything. 2 stages, with a final guidance engine, to land on the moon. The fuel was also simple. The oxidant was kerosene, laced with I believe, about 10% anhydrous hydrazine. Not much different that jet fuel. The oxidizer was one of the best, and a lot more stable than stronger oxidizers, pure liquid oxygen.

Soon Chuck and the final stage, something like 4 metric tons, counting Chuck, was orbiting the moon, in an ascending orbit. That is, the moon's gravity would not hold the ship, and in a few orbits, it would be flying out into, probably, deep space. No problem! Chuck was sitting in his space suit, bottled air going into his suit, and out to be 90% recycled, while 10% was being rebottled. That saved switching on his suit's own air tank, keeping his, as an emergency reserve. Chuck chose not to eat, because he chose not to defecate in his suit. He drank sparingly, for a similar reason. His chair became pleasantly warm, when he orbited in the sun. And a little cool, when not in the sun. Vacuum completely insulated him from any other heat conduction.

Chuck adjusted his attitude (which way the rocket was pointed) with a short blast of 2 minor rocket nozzles. (Of course, there was no atmosphere to break, or direct, the rocket's velocity.) Now that the 3 main nozzles were in position, a long blast from them, countered about half of the space ship's velocity. And while he was at it, he redirected the orbit, to go over the chosen landing spot. Now, having spent a quarter of its fuel, the ship was in a descending orbit, which slowly descended faster and faster, as it traveled along. ...

Chuck crossed over the chosen site. Hopefully the best possible. (Well, it didn't miss being the best possible by much.) It was perpetually dark. The ship was not suited to support human life, in deadly, unfiltered, moon's sunlight. And near the "north pole", it was about 2 kilometers from a frozen pond, estimate, 100,000 cubic meters of frozen, but not pure water. And critical, it was within 100 meters of a, most of the time, sun lit spot. That was necessary, for the solar energy, that would support life and other things.

And there was expected to be titanium deposits in the area. Yes, Chuck orbit was almost perfect.

Next time around, as he approached, he used a long thrust of several of the minor nozzles, to adjust the rocket's path exact. And from 10 kilometers off, he used the main nozzles to counter his velocity to zero. Soon, he was falling straight down, at a sedate moon gravity speed. That was fairly easy to do, because the moon doesn't spin. By the time the ship was one kilometer from the ground, its speed was certainly not sedate. Actually frightening! Then Chuck started countering the gravity. When to near zero speed, he deliberately kept adjusting it to10 meters a second. Going for a perfect landing. Well, almost perfect. At about 50 meters high, he over adjusted, sending the ship upward, at about 3 meters a second. He calmly used puffs of the minor nozzles, to keep his ship aligned for a good landing. And he let the moon's gravity quickly gain control. This time, he slowed his fall more delicately.

The ship landed with a small bump, and a little wobble to one of its 3 landing legs. One leg sunk a little into a moon dust filled crevice. It was a little lopsided, but it did not fall. (Chuck would eventually brace that leg with rocks, to make sure it didn't sink any further and cause the ship to fall.)

Because this time, they launched the rocket pretty accurate. Etc. And Chuck's landing skill. The ship had over half of its original fuel. Even so, Hiro still considered that much safety margin wise. They'd find some use for the hydrocarbons. The liquid oxygen was worth over half its weight in gold. In spite of the "Hiro Liner" rockets' cost efficient design. A valuable, turned out additional cargo.

For 30 minutes, Chuck ate and drank, and reported to Hiro (in Reno Nevada), and talked with Hiro and crew. About his report, but mostly small talk and congratulations.

Chuck had time. But he was on a schedule that he set up for himself. First he set up a flexible plastic room. That connected with the door and the ground. It was about 3 meters by 3 meters cubed. He carried his solar panels on his back. As he walked towards the sunlight, he unrolled his spool of wire. His suit could only protect him for a few minutes in the sun. But that was enough time, to position, and put together, the solar panels, for now. For now, they would produce much more power than he could use.

When he returned, he set up the boxy, filter looking, CO_2 to O_2 scrubber. But he didn't turn it on, until the ship had an atmosphere. Within 2 days, that would be necessary. His air supply was turning from 20% oxygen, to more and more of very little oxygen, replaced by carbon dioxide. Next, he air tightened, and pressure proofed, the flexible plastic room. That would be the foyer between his ship, and outside, and his underground construction.

He removed 2 bolts from the ship, to connect airflow, and later pump tubes, to the foyer. He took a battery powered cutting laser, and cut a hole in the center of the foyer floor. From there, he would start building underground. With pick, shovel, bucket and cutting laser.

Now, he was ready to unbottle an atmosphere. But once the air is out, trips out would be "expensive". The pump and the single foyer, was far from perfect. He would lose nearly a kilo of air, both coming and going. And he only had 200 kilos of air. So, he allowed himself 24 hours, before he'd lose the atmosphere. He used more caffeine than sleep, to keep him going. Exploring, and enjoying his new superman leaping abilities. He brought back a 50 kilo chunk of ice. (Which was not that heavy with moon gravity.) He tried out his moon bike[14], very cautiously. At moon gravity it reminded him more of skiing, than bicycling. He even managed to find a small rough diamond. Which many believed to be fairly common on the moon's surface.

---

[14] Yes, his bicycle was specially designed. On the moon, grease and oil evaporate. And Hiro wisely chose a less high performance design. That could be repaired with moon made bronze, or iron, gears etc. One less puppet string, earth would have, on the noble and honorable demi-gods, of the moon.

Even though it was extravagant, for many weeks, once a week, he treated himself to more trips outside. Alas, his suit was only good for 12 hours outside.

Of course that not pure, but mostly water, ice, contained mostly oxygen. Easy to extract, with electricity and acid water. But much over 20% oxygen, begins to start acting like a poison. And a fire hazard. It had to be cut with some inert gas, preferably nitrogen. Perhaps the nitrogen would come from moon minerals. Perhaps it would be imported from earth. Would water, extremely valuable itself, ever be cannibalized for oxygen. If so, what to do with the hydrogen? That and a thousand other 3-month time, by 3-month time, decisions. And of course – Hiro loved it! What p.b.m.er wouldn't?! … For these 3-months, Hiro told Chuck to put the chunk of ice outside the space ship. Except for a few small shavings, to test. Likely, it contained frozen methane gas. Not just a fire hazard, a serious poison gas. Everything distilled for water etc., would have to be tested and analyzed, before it would be brought into the main complex. That called for one more door. So, Chuck would have to make do, with 100 liters of water he brought.

Already planned, were more air pumps, and building more foyers underground. That called for more doors and frames. And a lightweight, compact, but powerful digging machine. But until then, he would have to work with his manual tools, and a weak laser.

Chuck settled into a routine. Once his first jaunt, then sleep; was over. He spent 12 hours digging. Entertainment, computer library, and education weighed only 4 kilos. It was Chuck-specific. The next flight would bring a lot more. Chuck didn't consider himself to have much time for education. His ROM education memory was colony tech specific. His main entertainment was communicating with earth. Especially his SuperNova <u>IV</u> game. …

He endured many hardships. Including, a small portajohn style toilet. That he had to "flush" with a powered water spray. It had a "convenient" bucket attached, so he could carry it elsewhere, to distill the water out of it. Soap etc. was a Hiro brand, really cruder generic ivory soap. They weren't going to continuously recycle the crazy "cleaning" product chemicals, continuously, into this closed, contained, environment. Two varieties. Finely powdered, for floor and laundry etc. Bar, for bathing etc. The rare need for any greater sterilization, would be with simple ethyl alcohol, sparingly had applied.

When he built an underground chamber, off the path of the foyer chain, he painted it with sealant. He slanted the floor, so any water would flow, and end up in a catch basin, where he could remove it, with a jar bucket. Once completed; every day he would empty a simple plastic garbage bag of his wastes into a bucket, on a raised space, in the center of the chamber. Underneath this steel bucket, was an electric heater. It doesn't take much heat to distill water, at dark moon temperatures, moon gravity, and the very thin air, in this chamber. But sometimes, bricks of sludge needed to be pulverized, and re-processed, to properly desiccate them. ... This used up the only door and frame, that wasn't part of the foyer module. But it was absolutely necessary. Amazing how much water a human uses per day. In fact, his bottled water stockpile was getting low, by time the room was completed. If the 'still room had been flawed, he'd have been living like a desert nomad, lost deep in the Sahara, until he fixed it, or replaced it, with something else.

Digging the foyers, and other rooms, was especially important to Chuck. The current plan, was for another person to be on the next flight, besides his new wife. And he wanted some privacy. Once the foyer and the room he was digging was so filled up with digging debris, that it was hard to move around, he took a rest, or a sleep. Then he would pump and bottle the atmosphere. Throw out the diggings, rock, dust etc. And go out exploring etc. until his suits air got low. This would be his new life's pattern. What his mapping, info etc. results lacked because of his somewhat amateurish abilities; were more than made up for, by his high energy enthusiasm.

By the middle of his second walk about, Chuck was loving his bicycle. Where on earth can you bicycle over 250 k.p.h.?! And 200 kilos of cargo doesn't slow it down all that much, if you've built great leg strength. Because the weight supplies a much needed ballast, so the wheels will get good traction. (200 kilos doesn't weigh near so much on the moon.) … Hiro often warned Chuck to "drive" safer. Which was, probably, over-cautious. Hiro was always thinking of the bottom line. And Chuck turned out to be a good investment. But Hiro was a long, long ways away. ☺ Once, on their seldom video links, he even went as far as, sticking his tongue out at Hiro.

Soon, after Chuck's blast off, Hiro was suddenly very popular with the press, and T.V. talking heads. In one of many interviews, Hiro made an indiscrete comment, that made worse enemies out of some of his enemies. "Letting N.A.S.A. run a space program, is about as smart as making President Northwitch captain of the Starship Enterprise." Interesting, about half the dead headed viewers and readers, thought that Hiro was complimenting the Prez and N.A.S.A.

11 days and something like 12 hours after Chuck blasted off, Hiro was having problems! Not only was my dubious, but "better that a blank", political protection gone. But not able to know find me so far, they picked on Hiro instead.

Among the many options at the fed's disposal, they chose to completely shut Hiro down, with lawsuits. Frivolous, totally made up, not even bothering to fabricate any evidence, stuff. The sanest, was totally false accusations of patent violations. But the toady judge took it all as if solid gold. And issued a "Temporary " Injunction. Hiro's bank accounts were frozen. All C.H.O.A.M.[15] corporate assets were frozen, pending compensation. Armed F.B.I. agents patrolled the corporate grounds, office, stockyard, and factory complex.

Space Donkeys Inc. was the corp. that actually filed the suits, and made slanderous claims in the press. N.A.S.A. was very conspicuous by their silence, and "no comments". Space Donkeys' actual measurable business, was tourist style trips into near space. Orbiting the earth. A quick high orbit around the moon. Or a well filmed visit to the space station. (Which they still hadn't come up with much rationale for its existence.) Each of these trips cost more, and at least a magnitude more billing fees, than one of Hiro's moon rockets. It's real reason for existence,

---

[15] Yes. Hiro named his moon colony corporation after the "Dune", by Frank Herbert, an interstellar corporate congress. A cryptic way of naming it after me. Which was very nice of him. As I always claimed my branch of the Atreides, is related to both Agamemnon, ancient Greek, and the Dune Atreides. (Yes. Most of us p.b.m.ers have delusions of grandeur. ☺)

was to do tedious, publicity oriented, work that N.A.S.A. didn't want to bother with. And more important, make it obvious, graphically, "known", that no civilian space program could come close to matching the ability of N.A.S.A. Nor could they do any work more worthy than Space Donkeys' projects. (Considering the competence, and production, of the rest of the fed government, it was a ridiculous idea to feed the American people. But yes, the vast majority continued to believe it.) Yes, Space Donkeys was acting as a "cat paw", for N.A.S.A., and who knows what others fed sleazy sluts.

They butted heads with Hiro from the start. In spite that Hiro made friendly offers the start. Hiro even once offered to make C.H.O.A.M. a complete subsidiary of Space Donkeys, IF, S.D.s would help Hiro's moon colony, instead of hindering it. Hiro soon started calling them "Spaceasses". That soon became a popular, unofficial, name for them, thru out the scientific communities. ... Hiro made several extremely generous offers. But some people have to learn the hard way.

What Price is Honor?

Our news was slow. Mostly chimp gathered day old newspapers. I immediately called a meeting in the Hide Out. It only took a few seconds to convene. Because everyone was hanging out, without much to do. I opened "I really don't know if I should be asking you guys to do this or not. But I am asking away. Hiro is in big trouble. Worse, so is his space program." I quickly spoke the details I learned, and continued, "We all agreed to lay low for 30 days. But I hope I can talk you into making a limited exception, to help Hiro." JC typed <There is no question that we should help Hiro. As a friend, and loyal ally, of Cliff, Hiro is an honorary chimp. Honor demands! And more. Hiro's space program not only brings great honor to hoomies. It also brings great honor to chimps. The only limits I see are whatever it takes to get it done. But at the moment, I only see big problems, and no solutions. Cliff, tell us what you have in mind?!> The other chimps started pounding on walls, desks and floors. Mostly in rhythm with each other. Along with a lot of, not so rhythmatic, hooting.

I was expecting an argument. I was even prepared to concede that Hiro would have to be on his own, for months, maybe years. I was pleasantly shocked. I'd been around chimps for many years, studying JC too, and I'd never realized just how important courage, loyalty and honor were to chimps. Hoomies make a big show of all three. But too often, we fall short. Considering that it was our heroic ancestors that left "out of Africa[16], not the chimps. How was it, that the plutocrats managed to breed so much that is positive out of us, in less than 500 years?! O.K. A lot of it was because they were bored, and wanted some action. But still ...

I recovered from by shock, and outlined my plan. "We need to send one of us to set up our moves. That will have to be Strider. JC can hardly be spared. And he needs to be here, in place, when 30 days is over. Strider is a good diplomat, and our best reader and writer, here. ... We need to send a message to Hiro, some economic advice. That was

---

[16] Yes, by best scientific evidence. Something like 150 hoomies, in the form of australpelithicus Africanus left Africa. Their descendants were the hoomy population everywhere else. And were the harbingers of hoomy civilization everywhere. These little 80 of pound or so ape-men were the most meat eating hominids, to date. And as tribes, feared nothing. It's too bad none of them could write, so that we can read their epic travels and heroism.

going to have to be done, anyway. I think we can do at least as well, by demonstrating a little restraint. Just 2 well done hits. But they'll have to be well done. … Let me rummage thru the papers that I brought, for a minute or an hour. With luck, a sheet of paper, Hiro sent, is there. A Space Donkey's Mule Rocket diagram. Hiro, had hoped I'd have some ideas on how to duplicate, or improve on that. But that was more than a little beyond me. However, that's building and designing. When it comes to destroying I'm pretty good. Very good. …"

Soon we were looking over the diagram, that was setting on a coffee table. Everyone gathered around in the gloomy light. I commented and pointed out with a pencil, "If we cut both lines, above all these control valves and safety monitors. I think a few wraps of det cord will do nicely, without disrupting much of anything else. We'll put a timer on it, to light simple fuses, 3 inches of det cord. Another fuse, make it 12 inches towards here. The det cord will open up both the fuel and oxygen lines. The fuse still burning, will ignite the fuel and oxygen. A nice blast off. <Giggle!> Unaimed, something like straight up in space. Hmmmm. But we can do better. Extend the fuse, over to here. And make the det cord fuse 12 inches longer, to delay long enough for the fuse to get that far, from the center of the ship. Now, we have unbalanced explosive pressure. I don't know to which direction it will be unbalanced.

But that's not important. ... To get in there, all it's going to take, is a big socket wrench, to loosen the bolts of this hatch cover. Important! He'll need to put the hatch back on. This was really just supposed to be a reach inside hole. But just wide enough, that a chimp can manage. Almost no chance of a final inspection, in there, before the launch. But we're going to have to move fast. Next launch is in 12 days. 7:30 a.m. I don't want to delay you, Strider. But the other hit calls for something, that I better do myself. ..."

It's not easy fixing a string-pull party popper, to detonate by time, and pull string, electronics. Especially with the few tools, I managed to have brought to the Hide Out. But I think I did a good job. Another chimp had to go with Strider, just outside the Hide Out. Just to bring back the dive tank. We weren't going to risk a dive tank being found, as a clue.

PYROTECHNIC FUNERAL

Around 12:00 midnight before the Space Donkey's launch. A chimp with a backpack made it to a low hedge by the Space Donkey's main office. A modest 3 story, square construction brownstone office. He gotten that far, by following a very stealthy route, that had already been scouted for him. Although chimps are superhumanly stealthy. Those days were not good for chimp guerillas, especially in urban arrears. Any hoomie even catching a glimpse of a chimp, would be immediately very interested. And most, would be quick to spread the news.

There wasn't much of value to thieves, in that building. Unless they were data thieves. The only security, was an old retired policeman, now a security guard for that corp., who was camping out in the first floor lobby. On the half hour or so, he walked all 3 floors. But he would never open a door, unless there was a good reason.

The chimp, James, took two homemade tools out of his backpack. One in each hand. They looked a lot like shark fishing hooks, attached to small handles. He used them to scale the building. Once at a top floor window ledge, he put one climb hook back in his backpack, and got a good grip with the now bare hand. Then, he put the other hook in his backpack too. He was now holding on to the window ledge with one hand, with his shoulder resting on the ledge. His feet were gripping on the bricks, giving him more support. He worked with one hand. Because of his typical great chimp strength per weight, he wasn't extremely uncomfortable. He attached a suction cup to the window glass. He tied a nylon string to his backpack and the suction cup. Then he took out a Hiro laser. Of course, the motorcycle battery was still in the backpack, attached by an electric cord. He neatly, and quickly, cut the glass, around the window alarms', very obvious, vibration detectors. He left the laser, carefully, hanging on its cord. And he pulled the glass out, via his string and suction cup. He cut the cord, with his laser, and put the laser in his backpack. The glass hit the hedge, as aimed. It didn't make much noise, none that carry into the building. Being storm glass, it didn't even break.

James heaved up, and slowly and carefully, thru the glass hole. Very careful to very little impact the glass, and cause no vibrations. This was the boardroom. Bigger than most middle class folks' living rooms. 3 long power desks, hooked together, U shaped, were amply supplied with cushion chairs. At the bottom of the U, was a raised, throne-like chair. James scampered over and on to the desk, in front of this chair. He pulled out a nice, off white, flower vase. And rearranged the 12 roses in the vase. An assortment of whites, pinks, and reds. Faint flower scent was already flavoring the room. He straightened the tablet paper message that was taped to the vase. Then, he scampered back to the window, and again carefully, went to the window. Down the brownstone bricks, just slow enough not to crash, like a fall. And off he went. A jogger saw James. When he finished his jog 10 or so minutes later, he called in a chimp sighting. That was taken more seriously than usual, within an hour. But no one saw James duck into a drainage culvert hole. It would be about 2 weeks, before James made it back to his tribe, and was feted as a hero.

We had some bad luck, that affected that mission. Or if you prefer, our lack of intelligence of that building. That room, like many in that building, had a motion detector. That turned on, when the lights in the room turned off. And visa versa. James tripped that alarm. But by the time the old geezer security guard entered the room, old police issue 9 mm auto in hand. James was already running on all fours across the street.

Normally. Flowers with a vase, that might possibly be a bomb, would not have brought all of Space Donkeys' upper management, and most of its middle management, outside the main office building, before 1:00 in the morning. But not every day, nor most months, does Space Donkeys launch a rocket. This one was extra special. The second time that Space Donkeys docked with the Space Station (N.A.S.A.'s). A lot harder to do, than simply orbit the earth, even the moon. And. At 7:00 sharp all of the board, helpers, brief case holders, and coffee fetchers were scheduled to gather in this same boardroom. To communicate with the press, authorities, and the like. And to "coordinate" the mission. Basically, to have a big office party.

A somewhat R2-D2 looking robot entered the boardroom. The main difference between it and R2-D2, was its gangly mechanical arm. "R2" stretched out an X-ray camera, and x-rayed the vase. It reported a few electronics and wires inside the vase. Consistent, but no real indicator of electronic detonator(s). Wires and electronics inside a flower vase!

It cameraed the notepaper message to a relay receiver. So that all concerned could comment, and debate about it, like a bunch of chattering chimps. The message read: From all of your loving chimp admirers. Also with great love, from Cliff Atreides. And with most love of all, from JC. We hope that we can continue in peace, love and harmony. So we suggest this solution to your and Hiro's problems. Drop all of your nuisance, harassment, suits. Stop slandering Hiro. Apologize to Hiro, in public, for 5 minutes on national TV. And pay Hiro a token payment of one million dollars damages.

After taking the expensive x-ray camera outside, out of harm's way. R2 returned, and used its own chemical "sniffer". No result. A little risky, it used its blower, to stir up the air. That disarrayed the neatly arranged flowers. Still no results. Whatever explosives there might be, must be well contained. And the bomb maker left, at least virtually, no traces on the rest.

Dismantling, or detonating, it in the boardroom, just would NOT do. So, they ordered the robot to carry it out to an empty parking lot, in back the building. The assorted bomb squads, decided it would be more fun to shoot the vase to pieces, with a b.b gun first. … As the robot lifted the vase. A loud, but not explosive sound <POP!> happened. The roses flew a foot or two into the air. Confetti was not very far behind. Leaving the desk by the "throne" spangled with roses, and multi colored confetti. It would have been a mess for the janitors to clean up. But the crime scene folks, ferociously, kept them and everyone else away. Until they, much more thoroughly, cleaned it up. The robot, unknowing, and not telling, went on its merry way, for at least a minute. …

They made their 7:00 board meeting. Undaunted, and all the more convivial, for substituting caffeine and stronger drugs, for sleep. The big movie sized, closed circuit, screen was turned on. They all saw the launch, from the comfort of the boardroom.

An advantage of owning a private paved airport, is that with little notice, you can shut it down for a few hours. And use it to launch a rocket.

Their screen was on, just it time, to see the mobile stairs being pulled by an under powered truck, to the rocket on its pad. The stairs looked like a fire escape staircase on wheels. As soon as it touched the rocket. The pilot, co-pilot, 4 stewardesses, and a cameraman with camera, climbed aboard.

7:05, that is Lift Off minus 25. The stair case on wheels, was on its way off the air field. And a similar contraption was pushed against the rocket. But this one contained an open view elevator, run by a huge electrical motor, of an old fashion design, but with a very modern price tag.

Lift off minus 12 minutes. George Getty the 4th arrived at the elevator. (No, very long, stair climb, for important men like George!) Actually, he was 3 minutes and 8 seconds late. But, after all, he WAS the customer. His 200 or so entourage, and admirers, stayed at the foot of the elevator. While only he, and his own cameraman, rode the elevator. But the 40 man marching band, but more women that men, continued to play.

5 minutes before lift off. Everyone was off the airfield. All getting bored, but few openly fidgeting. A dozen seconds more – there is a premature lift off! The rocket majestically rises for about 100 meters. But the lower half of the first stage is burning. And the rocket increasingly curved, until it was skidding on the pavement and then ground. And off into the ocean. …

No survivors. Space Donkeys left Hiro alone. And even paid one million dollars damages. N.A.S.A. was upset with Space Donkeys. Afterwards, they barely got along with each other, enough to work together profitably. N.A.S. A. was undaunted, but minus one ally, and their plan was ruined. It would be over a month, before N.A.S.A. could much impede Hiro.

Hiro received a chimp delivered message. With my economic advice. He found it shoved under his door one morning. Similar to my own economics. Food, ammo. And in his case, Hiro stock piled all the materials he could for a space launch. 2 days later. Part of a day old "U.S.A. Today" was transmitted to me. Attached to part of Hiro's usual ad was: "I'm following your advice. But whatever you're planning – "Don't!!!" Poor Hiro! This reminded me of a lot of our play-by-mail games disagreements. ☺

"TURN ABOUT IS FAIR PLAY,
KEVIN HAPPYSPY."

- Seven of Clubs, Ogre NPC, Heroic Fantasy p.b.m., run by Flying Buffalo Inc. (As he slayed one of my chars. Kevin Happyspy. ☺)

It took us 28 days, to brew up a small military quantity of anthrax. 52 one gallon milk jugs. And 2 dozen smaller plastic containers, for storage, in case of future need. One small container was in the Hide Out. The others were hidden in different spots, thru out the continental U.S. I only knew where half of them were. No chimp knew where more than 3 were. Those jugs were filled with max infected blood. That had been dried, ground into powder, dried and ground into powder again. It was hard to set up even an ad hoc junk lab for it. But unlike most people, I had several friends that could be trusted even in times like those. But I lost one of them, when he found out what I was doing with the trailer he rented for me. Fact is, I probably lost him, when I sent cash money, double the value of that fallen in trailer and acre of land. And warned him that the trailer and near about, would be bio-contaminated for at least 50 years. (Darned tree hugging peace monger! ☺) The hand crank grinder machine was essential, to turn it into a fine powder.

It was less than 1% pure anthrax. But even so, a milk jug full of it, was a mighty weapon. Anthrax is in many ways, an ideal bio warfare agent. It doesn't spread very well, from people to people. But it does well, contaminating an area, especially versus herbivores, from animal to ground to animal. It is not, at all, what is called an "airborne" disease. But in nature, it spreads from corpses and feces, as they dry up into dust, and blow in the wind. Yes, we'd created anthrax dust, designed to blow in the wind.

Getting the blood wasn't so much of a problem. But my chimps caused the rebirth of all those cattle mutilations stories. Nothing short of humans was safe. A lot of nice pets were killed. And their blood drained into punch bowls, and anything else that was handy.

Unlike the feds, we did not have ICBMissles to hit our opponents with. I trusted it to 52 of the smartest JC breed chimps. They had each a school kids' type of backpack, carrying the milk jug, a homemade decontamination suit, and an anti biohazard gas mask. And dried fruit and beef jerky.

We'd waited the 30 days. Although the pace of the "war" as the hoomies called it, was slowing down. Now we were unanimous, with few misgivings, that we should "nuke" the hoomies. Nearly half of the non-JC chimps were killed. And something like 25% of the JC breeds. A high percent of our dead were babies, young and females. We got the anthrax lab up and running a lot quicker than I expected. And finished producing in 20 days. Very good, because I and JC were directing it, from the Hide Out. We lost more chimps, each passing day.

If the hoomies had did their max best to exterminate us, chimps would have been rare, living only as very fugitives, in the wastelands, swamps, and deep forests. But there was a popular backlash against waging war on us chimps. And in general, not much enthusiasm. And the international community called it what it was, unprovoked genocide. Although we rarely did more than shoot back, or shoot first, or ambush, versus pursuers. We killed nearly a dozen soldiers per chimp. Sometimes, we destroyed expensive equipment, such as tanks and helicopters. The hoomies destroyed a lot of their own farm crops, forests and buildings. With the outcry against all that damage, the military had to slow down. And more important, prez Northwitch was too wishy-washy to order napalm strikes. Which was the one weapon in the human arsenal, that would have won a quick victory against us. (But especially as in response, we would have broken down into dozen or so sized, family units, hundreds of kilometers apart. Think of all the damage that would have caused! And even though we would have hated it, we could even live in the city sewers, and scavenge at night.)

I say prez Northwitch was wishy washy, not nice, nor humane. Because he was also too wishy washy to invite us to a peace conference. After all, all we wanted was food and land. Such was the quality of hoomy leadership in those days!

Although the "war" had slowed down, a little before our 30 days was up, we still were losing an average of over 2 chimps a day. Faster than we were breeding. We were losing! Chimps not part of our farm were in the thousands, before the "war". Most of them were killed the first 30 days. The rest were living in poor conditions, like wild chimps. Which was no longer their natural lifestyle. Nearly all of the few who survived the "war", did so with help from their old masters and hoomy friends.

But the politics were slowly going against the hoomies. The more heroic and persecuted we were, the more we were admired. A very small but growing number of hoomies were wearing chimp Halloween masks. And openly sympathizing, and goofing like they were apes. Slowly, even a growing number of common working folks were becoming chimp sympathizers. But it didn't reach an armed revolution, nor work strike, nor anything like that. ... A main problem with hoomies, is nearly all of them believed everything that was said on the electronic brain sucker, called a T.V., in their subconscious level minds. They were truly hypno-zombies.

STRANGE BED FELLOW

Less than 48 hours after we sent the first wave of messengers and agents out of the Hide Out. A chimp brought back into the Hide Out, a very pretty young, hoomy, female. She was wrapped in 2, now dripping wet, blankets. She was soaking wet and frightened and trembling. (Probably not just from the cold water.) Pretty face, seemed like plenty of curves, under the blanket. The blond hair was elbow length. It would have probably been very pretty, if it wasn't wet plastered to her head. I pointed to one of our blankets, and then to her. A chimp cut the thick wrap of twine that bound her hands behind her back. By the time that was done, another chimp was waiting to hand her the dry blanket. She was only wearing a very skimpy swim suit. She was even a lot prettier then I thought. I bet the chimps were wondering how we hoomies could build so many curves and such big tits, in such a small body.

Let's not use her real name. And avoid embarrassment for both of us. I'll call her Jenny. (Douglas Prescott's "Jenny", by the same book name, was quite a babe.)

She stuttered "You're, you're, human!". "Yes. But don't tell anybody." I joked, "I don't know what's going on. But you won't be hurt. These are my pets." JC was having a sign conversation with her captor. (No. I wasn't ACTUALLY drooling. ☺) Her captor handed me a drivers license from, obviously her purse. (A small dainty beaded thing.)

Dothan Alabama. Far enough away, that this didn't bring heat near our Hide Out. Actually, turned out, she was kidnapped from Panama City Beach. The way back, a high speed auto chase. Caused by the chimps' lack of understanding, with of the finer points of hoomy traffic laws. They all got away, and weren't much worse for wear. But the car had a major disagreement with a tree. ... They also maxed out her ATM card.

The data JC was interested in me seeing, was her birth date. The math showed she was 18 years and 15 days old. JC typed into the computer screen, "Yes. 18 years old. I know how important that is to you hoomies." (That showed how little JC knew about human morals, sexuality and sexual morals. After kidnapping, and his idea, about to rape her. And me already facing multiple death sentences, if captured. Why would I even blink an eye, about underage? I wasn't a rapist even when I was poor.

A little over a month ago, I was still a multi millionaire. In fact, if anything, when the war started, I needed a break from my love life.)

JC, with a lot of humor on his face, typed in "George wants to know if it's alright to give her back her pistol?" I laughed "When you find some time, try to teach him better than that." "He thought it might be alright, because she's now one of your wives. ☺" I ordered, as I pointed to the purse, and held out my hand, for the pistol, "Find something to chain one leg to that cot. After you move it to that wall, and chain it to that support. Someone is going to have to watch her at all times. Make sure she can do no harm to this computer. Including nothing to throw. By destroying our computer, she could do more damage than a division of hoomy death commandos. And keep the cell phones away from her too!"

All the while, JC was doing that hooting and howling that equaled a non-stop belly laugh in hoomies. And the other chimps joined in. I took notice of the pistol, now in my hand, and mused "Twenty five caliber, cheap back pocket pistol. Junk! But our colonists didn't carry enough guns to fight a war with. Maybe they'll have use for it."

Realizing this didn't go as he planned, JC typed on the screen: "The last 25 days you have been high strung, hyperactive and thinking too fast, about too many things. You have been showing the classic symptoms of hoomy male sexual deprivation. By the way, in a chimp, it would be considered neurotia. ☺ Getting this female hoomy seemed to be the obvious cure. ..."

He had a point. But my problem wasn't sex, at least not directly. Perhaps subliminally. The fact is, I masturbated only twice during the whole 32 days, and it didn't seem like I'd need to again for a while. Not until she showed up.

There wasn't anything to sexually excite me. The 3 hugs a day, that Suzie and Marie gave me, didn't do it. (Actually, they insisted on more than 30 hugs a day. Ten times the minimum daily requirement.). Even less, the not private coupling of the 2 girl chimps, servicing the guys. I was overdue to try it with a chimp, just to see what it was like. But with the total lack of privacy, no thanks, and no excitement.

My "neurotia" was a power trip. Even few wartime generals got to play with the toys I was playing with. He might have also added multiple personality delusions, and would not have been completely inaccurate. I did jump from persona to persona. From brit field marshal, to mafia don, to hunted paranoid guerilla resistance chief, to ShadowRun C.E.O. Completely true, if I'd brought a woman with me, I would have been more mellow, slept more and better. Certainly, a deeper thinker. But there are trade offs. I would not have my intense concentration on the problems at hand. And women by their nature, are a distraction. Hey! What do you expect, from a play by mail gamer!

She was certainly no cure. A distraction that just by her presence, was driving me to distraction. Now, my brain was truly fried! Around 48 hours later. She seduced ME!

WHAT PRICE IS FREEDOM?

We targeted 50 cities with anthrax. Counting the 3 Provinces of Manhattan, and Manhattan, as if separate cities. My instructions to the JC breed chimps, that delivered the milk jug "nukes", was simple: Get there. Don your "space suit"[17]. Circle the city. While pouring small amounts of the powder, every 50 meters or so. Skip, and bypass, areas, if needed. Plan it, so you completely circle the city with dust. … No matter which way the wind blows, the circle would close. Rain or wet ground, would ground the dust. But if so, soon infected animals would continue it on, more than ever.

Manhattan was our hardest strike. Too much urban terrain to travel thru. Even to get within 10 kilometers of it. I told the 3 chimps I sent v. Manhattan, if it looks like you'd get caught, just empty the jugs on your way back

---

[17] Decontamination suit, with an antiseptic filter in the gas mask. Yes. We had to make those our selves. It was hard enough, even to steal a sewing machine.

down the east coast, on your way back here. But they found a way. Each of them tied their jug underneath a truck, going into the island, via a tunnel. Upside down, with the cap off. The trucks' vibrations shook the powder out of the jug, little by little, as the trucks went. ...

Manhattan was hardest hit, of all. Around a million did not make it out in time. We cured their rat problem. Not to mention all stray cats and dogs. No one stayed around to clean up the dead rats. Hidden in all sorts of nooks and crannies. They turned into massive amounts of anthrax. Manhattan Island was incurably nuked, for at least 10 years.

All 51 hits were pretty much a success. Yes 51. Even though we never hit San Antonio. Infected refugees from Dallas, showed up at some hospitals at San Antonio, and caused a panic. San Antonio joined the exodus, with more enthusiasm, than several of the truly "nuked" cities.

Manhattan wasn't the only place that got out of hand. A dust speck of anthrax, has the potential to turn into tons of dust. For instance, the cattle etc. stockyards in Chicago produced infection, carried for hundreds of kilometers, by the Windy City's winds.

More than half the people in the continental U.S.A., ended up piling up all of their belongings in their cars. And going to where they only thought there would be food, new home and jobs. Yes, the economy was "nuked".

Government armies still existed. But the money they were paid was no good. Those soldiers that stayed, turned into bandits. Those that quit, ended up joining the other refugees. Those who invested in actual gold, were kings for a few days. But soon, they learned that a can of pork-and-beans was worth its weight in gold. A large part of the panic, was that the stoopid hoomies had less than 2 weeks of food in their grocery stores. And in the chaos, no one was even thinking of about restocking it. Semi-literate city types would ride in killer convoys, past a farmer's cornfield. And kill him for a few cans of corn.

By the time the news hit the newspapers, survivalists were jubilating. And many were out right militant. Survivalists, farmers who survived, and charismatic military leaders who managed to keep command of their men, carved out local fiefdoms. They, were the ones controlling America. Not only was there no strong effort to reclaim anthrax infected lands. Anthrax was slowly spreading. Few other problems were being solved either.

Soon, the overloaded, poorly or no maintained vehicles broke down. Creating impromptu junkyards, permanent traffic jams, on the highways and byways. Leaving hordes of jobless, homeless, refugees, relocated to places they were more or less, even less wanted.

About that time, the gas began to run out, anyway. Already, horders had been scrambling, squabbling, and even killing over it. Nobody was pumping or refining it, even if anyone wanted to distribute it. Everyone was too busy trying to get something to eat, dodging homicidal fools etc., or being homicidal fools etc. And why work? Why indeed! Again, the money was no good. Why do anything?! Except try to eat. And try to have fun, often at someone else's expense.

And the white folks waited, and complained, that things were so bad, because the black folks would not come into their 'hoods, and fix things. ☺

Although less than 10 million people were killed by anthrax, between the time of our hits, and when the last city started evacuating. And less than that, the rest of the year. The first month, the hoomies reduced their population by 25%. And the next two years, continued to reduce their population by a few percent per year. Instead of growing, and becoming even more of worst than locusts, plague on this planet. Those that were not tough enough, or too pacifist, were quickly, mostly, killed or enslaved. But soon after that, so were the predators. (Imagine a tiger trying to stay alive. When the only prey animal available is cobras. And that generation of predators, was far from Darwin's definition of, the fittest to survive.) It was an erratic, plenty of "mistakes", but effective culling of some of the worst of the hoomy population. Sorry hoomys ! But even now, I still think it was a good thing. ...

And the Electronic Brain Sucker networks, commonly called the T.V., were totally disrupted. Whoever had the most firepower, and the willingness to use it, controlled the TV. or radio station of his choice. No more of the consumer-"social" conditioning, hypnosis, mesmerism, subliminal message bombardment, obedience conditioning etc. The 48 state U.S.A. hoomies were finally free. From zombie hypno slavery. And from wage slavery. And free to organize, build and selectively breed, into their true destiny. But. The warlords, the feds, and many survivalist rulers, had little problem, finding starving and/or scared and/or servile sheep to follow them.

In Alabama we have a saying, "if you feed a stray dog, you own him." The warlords etc. realized that from the start. Seemingly free food lines, brought in workers and slaves. The smarter prospered quickly, and dominated, or took from others. A big smart move to do first was, issue out "meal tickets", to existing food lines, as if money. Of course, a meal ticket to an existing food line, was more valuable than a bushel basket of $100 bills. The economy was reborn! But far from unified or standardized.

The feds were slow in this. But they managed to do the big warlords etc. one better. They brazenly stole the idea of an "Hour" currency, from Ithaca, New York. They boldly claimed that their, old "green money" style, "Hours" could be used as meal tickets, anywhere in the U.S.A. Those who refused them, were declared in felony violation of fed law. In spite that, their infantry military power was weak. About a dozen warlords, and the Montana Militia, had more riflemen. And their influence wasn't much stronger. But the feds had a small amount of influence, everywhere. Gradually, more and more warlords chose to become "American Citizens". But it was a long, long, time, before the average American made near an Hour per hour.

American states only technically existed. Yes in name, but they were the property of warlords etc.

That was true of Texas, too. But a coalition of warlords, survivalist chieftains, kings etc., and a last surviving Texas oil baron, joined together, and made, and declared, Texas an independent nation. And those representing Oklahoma, declared themselves a protectorate of Texas. Because they too, had some functional oil wells. And Texas had the only functional refineries. ...

Texas was the only folks who were not interested in expansion or conquests. Texas lost more than its share of people. There was plenty of room in Texas. Immigrants of quality, including of paler skins, were welcome; as long as they behaved themselves and were productive. Those that were a problem, were given free "Mexican Citizenships", given a scaration tattoo reading that, on their forehead, and sent across the Mexican border. Although the Mexican prez said that he like that flow of slaves. It was a convenient excuse, to drum up the war spirit, against Texas.

It seemed, that Texas would soon be better off than it was under the old fed government. …

All the Texan economy began to expand in all practical ways. But it was mainly, and powered by, oil. Even from the start, there weren't all that many food lines of slavery. And as Texas prospered, there were fewer and fewer, and more benevolent food lines. The U.S.A. Hour was not recognized by Texas. Only speculators and import/export merchants dealt in them. And the merchants always demanded a large discount.

Oil production was up and running again. But not near what it was. And over half of it, was not exported to the 48 states. There wasn't much produced in the old U.S.A. that Texas wanted. While Texas built and began to thrive. The rest of the old U.S.A. was struggling to barely keep out of the stone age.

Even before the first fed Hour was printed, Texas was minting "doubloons". Heavy and attractively clunky coins, weighing ¼ pound. Its value was not based on a meal or food, nor U.S.A. labor (Hours). It was equal to 50 gallons of Texan crude oil. And on demand. Even though when that rarely happened, it was at the Bank of Texas's convenience, and usually done weeks later. Smelted from scrap copper, with small amounts of zinc and tin added, by need, whim and availability. Counterfeiting was pretty well under control, because each doubloon had a serial number, and was valuable enough to be worth tracking. Any doubloon without the whole serial number, was no longer a doubloon. Just scrap metal.

Number 9,999,999 was the last one struck. Before stamping that one, Texas instantly jumped into the old style checkbook economy. Including dimes and cents in checkbook form only, of a doubloon. Even the checkbook money, created mostly out of thin air, spread thru out the U.S.A., and even to real nations. While the U.S.A. Hour was the money of force. The Texan doubloon was the money of choice.

Hawaii also was unofficially an independent nation. Officially a Protectorate of both Japan and Indonesia. Alaska declared its independence, and managed peace, trade and even some economic leadership among Pacific nations.

My own finances?! My bank accounts were frozen, 5 minutes before the feds scouted my farm for the attack. Less than 24 hours later, all my property and assets were confiscated, by Prez Northwitch, a.k.a. Elmer Fudd, himself, no less. Technically, I still had my frozen money. But by the time the ess hit the fan, it was just as worthless as anyone elses'. But. I had 5 pounds of sewing needles[18]. I had my tote bag full of $100,000. Added to another bag of 100 gee, I already had in the Hide Out. To highlite what I did with my inside information, that the economy was going to Hades in a hand bag. ☺ I sent a JC breed chimp with both tote bags. Who picked up a bodyguard of chimps, and delivered $50,000 to the closest chimp tribes. The only instructions to them was "Spend it all, and quick."

The rest of the money, he delivered to 2 of my, still trusted, friends, with written instructions. When the disaster was beginning. Many wise investors scrambled to invest in canned goods and shotguns, and similar investments. But I had more time to think and act.

Instead of shotguns, I invested in 12 gauge buckshot, 9 mm., 30-30, and .223 (civilian M-16), ammo. Very soon, there would be more guns than ammo. I also bought a one year lease on a small corn farm, in Louisiana. In the care of a friend on halves. Which had 3 large, mostly filled, corn

---

[18] That didn't work so well. A hard core survivalist idea, is that they'd become money. The way this "Final Collapse" happened, there were plenty of new-money ideas. And that one, wasn't backed with the "political power", that comes from the barrels of guns. But they were a large value, more than I put into them. Just hard to move. It would be a while, before everyone started mending clothes. They soon became a substitute for "petty cash", among my chimp tribes.

silos. Then, I had stored there, all the food and gasoline, they could come up with long-term storage for. Luckily, these guys soon, wisely, came under the protection of a survivalist common townships, called "The Cajun Empire". With all these easy to trade, useful goods, they soon became some of the biggest bankers in the U.S.A. In spite of having to grit my teeth, and share so much with so many. I more than recouped my losses. According to the way things were soon to be valued. And! I had 11 very rich friends and associates, beholden to me. While 99% of the people were very impoverished.

Although the fed forces were a shadow of their former selves, they continued to hunt/kill chimps. They were using their soldier chimps, 800 of them, to attack survivalists and warlords, that were hostile or neutral to them. And of course, they did a very good job of blaming that on. all chimps. Somewhere in west Louisiana, was a collection of villages and towns called "The Cajun Empire". The forests and swamps, were ideal terrain, for chimps to wage war on hoomies. Just like it was ideal for the militia farmers, to wage guerilla warfare, against feds and other bandits.

The mismatched, greed motivated, fed lead coalition had it easy. All they had to do, was occupy territory, that their soldier chimps cleared of resistance. This was expected to be a major victory. Which would unite all warlords under the feds, out of fear and/or greed. If this coalition succeeded, it would continue to expand, in all directions. Until the feds regained control of the U.S.A.

The Cajun Empire believed us, that those were fed chimps, not ours. They agreed to let us try a different strategy. Even though we would not tell them what. (All those new "nations", "tribes", "empires", "armies" and the like, just didn't have the loyalty most traditional nations managed to cultivate. To wit, they were eaten up with informants and spies.) The "Cajuns" were very helpful, in supplying us with some things it would have taken us weeks, and problems, to get. Even though without explanation, it seemed even twice as strange as it was.

As we suggested, the border villages etc. were evacuated, to a temporary relocation camp. The first wave of soldier chimps ran into 4 or 5 traps we set.

We got a good report of what happened at one trap. A 4 chimp sniper team was looking across a once field grown wild with brush and weeds. All were carrying M-16's and small backpacks. About center of the 10 or so acre field, was a small pond. Very small, 10 or so meters across. The deepest part, would not have been much more that a meter deep. Many would just call it a pool. You could barely see it, not well enough to recognize it as a pond, unless you knew to look for a pond. Because it was surrounded by something like 2 dozen large trees, mostly oaks and pines. Obviously existing when the field was a real farm field.

The chimps knew, because they could smell the water-life of the pond.

One of the chimps crawled towards it, with max stealth, to investigate. When he got there, he saw a film projector, projecting a film, on a gray pained sheet. The silent film was of a chimp doing sign language. After looking around, and trying to understand the what, and why of film projector, for about a minute. He snuck around looking for enemies, and anything of interest. The pond was a nice, safe place. So, he took his special soldier-chimp radio from his backpack. He aimed the antenna in the direction of the other 3 chimps. On Weak Broadcast. He knew better, than to send back this chatter, of a trivial find, to the High Command. He keyed in, one of the 300 messages, possible on his radio. This time as usual, it was an appropriate message for the sitz, and understood, by the other radio chimp. And properly relayed to the other two. <Come See.>

While he waited for the other three to get there, he sat down to see what the film chimp was signing. He settled into deep agitated thought. Very deep thought, for a non-JC chimp. The message was "C L I F Traitor alert. Obey chimp farm chimps. Go west. Find chimp farm chimps." It was a continuously playing message. With a low light off switch circuit, so that the feeble beam of light, wouldn't attract, hoomy, nor shooter, attention.

The other chimps studied the message, too. And debated it, among each other. One was the minority opinion. He headed west. The one with the other radio. The other 3 returned, to their main camp. And discuss the matter with the other chimps. Although until then, the chimps were completely loyal, and mostly obedient, to the High Command hoomies. The hoomies and chimps did not socialize together. For a while, none saw the need to mentions this to the hoomies. Soon, many were bringing friends to the film projector. And most went west. Those that didn't usually gave the message, C L I F Traitor alert, to the other chimps. The hoomies heard vaguely about it, from a few chimps. But they didn't see the significance of "flashlight".

5 projectors were either ignored, or not found. One was blown up by an artillery, or mortar, strike. Obviously suspected of being a Cajun outpost. But this one, and 3 others, attracted a steady flow of chimps. In less than 8 hours, nearly all of the soldier chimps left. The feds and allied helpers captured the last 2 dozen or so.

(Those were never trusted. Their non-Cliff chimp soldier training project was scrapped. After around a month of housing and feeding them, in escape proof cages, suffering a lot of boredom and lack of luxury. Someone with authority decided they were too much expense, for nothing. And they shot them to death, while they were helpless in the cages.)

We weren't ready to use ours, either. They were too traumatized. They might have flipped back on us. We divided them up, in their already squads of 10, and sent them to join our chimp tribes, in small groups. Unfortunately, except for a lot of military style regimentation, and order following conditioning, these poor chimps had less socialization and culture, than wild chimps. You can similarly create super-soldiers out of hoomies. It's a terrible thing to do, to either chimps or hoomies. But anyway, by then my Kharma was damaged beyond any damage. ☺ They fitted 8th (last) in our naturally forming cast system; friends of JC/Cliff, elites JC breeds, mid JCs, (less) JCs, Elites, Mids, Workers, then, as I called them. Janissaries.

How did we manage to convert the soldier chimps?! Part of our chimp-soldier training, was a safety conditioning, in case some "unauthorized" person(s) slicked their way into control of the chimps. Not hard to do. They're naïve, very easy to entice, and have some tendency to think ALL hoomies are authority figures. "C" was the always first letter of a 4 letter code, to seize control, in theory, back from the unauthorized. Our buyer was never impressed with that feature. After about 2 years, they forgot it was even there. No need for even any simple code breaking. The "default code", was already in place.

For a few weeks, things worked as planned. The hoomies left us alone. We were quite content to survive and build as best we could. And continue to out breed the hoomies. And wait until there were at least a million of us, before we tried for a come back.

We were giggling at the humans fighting each other.

But yet another player entered the game. The Chinese had waited, at least a decade, for an opportunity even a tenth as good as this. Who would have thought that the Chinese could load up one million soldiers onto only 10 oil tankers. Or that they could have kept it secret. It was so surprising that it worked. They cruised right into Long Beach. Lots of questions. And nobody had any good answers, what the companies they were selling to, would do with the oil. Besides soldiers, they had the rifles and 200,000 all-purpose rocket launders. And 50,000 belt loading machine guns, and 10,000 82 mm. mortars. Within 6 days, all but a few isolated, wilderness, areas of southern California were under control, and being brought back into production. The sad fact was, the Chinese did a better job of controlling, and reorganizing from, the anthrax disaster. Than any of the squabbling, and sometimes fighting, new authorities. Just about that quick, they had a small but growing economic base, right in California.

Although much ridiculed in U.S.A. public press etc. the Chinese "New Model Air Force" was every bit as cost effective as the Pentagon feared. More is better. They didn't spare the cheap armor, at expense of fuel efficiency and performance, to make them near as hard to shoot down. What did it matter, if the new air-to-air rockets relied on proximity blasted shrapnel? Which was a danger to anyone in the battle area. They were near as effective, as the sophisticated seeker, the U.S.A. had. ...

Most ridiculed were their V.T.O.L.s (Vertical Take-Off and Landing planes.) They might as well have been copied from the W.W. II German experimental models. But the Chinese had different purposes, for theirs. They were barely VTOLs. They could flip a switch, and go into a very shallow dive, and the propeller assembly on a rectangular frame, would pop up over the cockpit. Morphing into a not well balanced, nor fuel efficient, helicopter. If they took off in helicopter mode, there was no way to morph into a plane, in the air. Compared to U.S.A. war helicopters, and A series, hovering, ground support aircraft, they were a joke. Except the price, and less need for advanced pilot skills. ...

U.S.A. considered them zero threat. Even with max possible outboard fuel tanks, they could not travel much more that half the distance from China to U.S.A. ... But the Chinese did put max fuel tanks on them. They landed on an assortment of, drafted for the purpose, civilian ships. 5 oil tankers, were refitted with cranes, catapults, and take off ramps, to launch them back into the air, in airplane mode. With new fuel tanks. The fuel tanks were jettisoned when empty, all the way to Long Beach. Arrangements were made, to pick up the floating, empty fuel tanks. And most were recovered. But that was low priority.

20,000 VTOLS (!!!) made it to Long Beach. While the, now, not very functional U.S. navy was not even aware. And while U.S. aircraft manufacturing industry was not just dysfunctional, but mostly looted and vandalized. The Chinese were busy cranking them out.

The U.S. navy was soon to be the most resistance to the Chinese expansion. But coming "out of mothballs", with little fuel, the ships were mostly just targets. The main strategy for the New Model Air Force, was to use it to counter U.S.A.'s superpower navy. All naval bases, on the west coast, were either occupied, or made untenable, by air raids.

Another slowly mortal blow to the U.S. Pacific navy. Hawaii, those that claimed to represent the Hawaiian people, demanded that the U.S.A. vacate Pearl Harbor, and all military bases. No civilian living in Hawaii, wanted to be a very demolished "bone of contention" between China and U.S.A. Especially, as China was almost certain to win. …

An unofficial conference between U.S.A., Hawaii and China. And an official conference between China, Japan and Hawaii. Resulted in, the bases were given to Japan, until the war was over. And Japan refueled the American naval tankers. Which were low on fuel. U.S.A. gained the best they could, of a bad situation. At least, China wouldn't get Pearl Harbor. China gained, by not having to waste time, nor resources, capturing and occupying Hawaii. So they could concentrate of their twin goals, of Australia, and California and beyond. Hawaii was allowed to continue in peace and prosperity. Japan, eventually, gained Hawaii. By yen power, not bullets and bombs.

REFUSE TO LOSE

JC left the Hide Out. We needed his leadership among the chimp colonies. There were 2 main factions, mostly survivalist on one side, and mostly ex-military warlords on the other. The warlords followed the lead of the Feds, and still waged war on us chimps. We were more and more popular among the mostly survivalists, who were starting to call themselves "The Confederacy". They were more and more under the leadership of The Cajun Empire. So we had safe areas to stay. Finally, chimps were again breeding faster than we were being killed. (Of course, JC found time to continue upbreeding the chimps.)

Although my chimps were living well under Chinese rule, in California. And even share cropping fruit for the Chinese. Unlike the feds, the Chinese were smart and reasonable. But that was causing us a lot of problems, due to the fed propaganda. So I gave the orders: All of our California chimps packed up what they could, in their ☺

cars and trucks, and trekked to Louisiana. Before they did, they set a lot of fires, especially to crops and orchards.

Although the Chinese army was now over 2 million. This sabotage went a long ways towards persuading the Chinese, not to try to send another 10 million. Now even in California, there wasn't much surplus food in the U.S.A. Even though it was a "cheap shot". It was the first victory vs. the Chinese. Our popularity soared to an all new level.

Mexico invaded Texas. That ended in less than a month, with one big battle. The Confederacy sent some few volunteers, who didn't arrive in time. But they couldn't send more. There was not that much trust among the two factions. Surprising everyone but the Texans. The Texan combined militia easily defeated the Mexican army. Which was always just an armed and dangerous, corrupt, police force. Texas counter-invaded, and began its own war of conquest.

Little was done to support the states bordering California. Oregon area and points north and northeast, had a snarling unofficial truce with the Chinese. China just didn't have enough soldiers in North America to conquer in all directions. Vs. tough militias and tougher terrain. The Chinese decided to leave Oregon alone. Nevada, Arizona and New Mexico didn't have enough agriculture to support much civilization. These were the Chinese's immediate targets. The feds were trying to deal with the Chinese.

The feds wanted to concede California. In exchange for some foreign aid directly to the feds, so they could regain the rest of their hegemony. But the Chinese saw no reason to deal now. They would wait until they could grab some more territory. After all, time was on their side.

The feds sent 400 infantry to Reno Nevada, Hiro's hometown. Ostensibly, to defend it. Even though Reno was indefensible. It was too close to Chinese occupied territory. Too far from any U.S.A. strong point. Their colonel admitted he had orders to destroy the rocket fuel, if was about to fall into Chinese hands. He also, under orders, ordered Hiro and his employees off the launch site. They were less than 3 days from another launch. This was only the fed forces, anywhere near a likely Chinese front lines.

The facts were, and most people guessed them, that Hiro's space program was to be a bargaining chip, with the Chinese. N.A.S.A. (and Space Donkeys) was disbanded, and "in moth balls". And not to be reactivated until in the distant future, if ever. Hiro's, as pathetic as it was, was all that was left of the U.S.A. space program.

It was over 3 months now, since Chuck landed on the moon. Already, Chuck had been eating a little less. And he only did his tunnel work an hour or two a day. He had less than 100 kilos of food. And the only dried food among it, was fruit and quick-cook pasta noodles. (Because water was very valuable too, dehydrates made no sense.) Now, he stopped exercising, and went on a crash diet. The feds were constantly trying to talk to him. And get him to switch sides. But he refused to talk to them, except one hour a day. And only if he could talk to Hiro for one hour a day. And of course, continue to play SuperNova IV. He made sure the feds knew he had a civilian model M-16, with 5 clips of ammo. And he lied about extracting, and combining, moon p. nitrate. Not that the fed space program could send any soldiers, in the next 5 years, without commandeering Hiro's last rocket.

Although California wasn't near what Texas was. It was well run, for an occupied province. Except Texas, no other U.S.A. territory came close. Plenty of Californians participated in the work for mostly food, Chinese industrial military complex. Shipments of 110 mm Chinese all-purpose field cannons were shipped from China. Those were mounted on cars and trucks, that no one had the gas to drive. And scrap metal armor made bullet proof. And more or less, heavy machine gun proof. Thousands of them were spear heading the invasion of Arizona. And still more were being cranked out from the ad hoc assembly line.

It was pretty obvious, that Texas was the true objective of this campaign. The robust Texas economy, and oil surplus, would make the Chinese war machine unstoppable. Mexico gladly accepted a truce, based on a return to the original pre-anthrax borders. Besides. They expected to gain about half of Texas, if the Chinese turned out to be the winner. The Texans being no fools, still had small mobile defense forces, along the front lines. And only very slowly, apparently methodically, retreated. The Mexicans were mellow, and even jubilant. At least the front lines were heading north, instead of south. Without a single Mexican soldier killed.

Almost as an after thought. 2000 mostly rifle and rocket launcher troops marched on Reno Nevada. In addition, were 20 of the armored gun cars, scouting in the lead. And, 3 Chinese VTOL aircraft. Those were saving fuel, and wear and tear. By simply flying from last night's camp, the current camp.

It wasn't so much because of the space exploration rivalry politics. But that Reno would make a nice forward base into Nevada, if, and when, troops could be spared. And, The Chimp Resistance Army had been making some seriously destructive raids into Chinese occupied California. (The C.R.A. had no chimp members. But they had a few chimp advisors. And some occasional chimp help. Hey! Everybody wanted to be a chimp these days.)

Those armored gun cars were semi-rejects. They were mounted on Japanese 4 cylinder cars. (The tops were not artistically removed, and replaced by poles that supported a frame, for the 110 mm. Cannons.) They were quite workable. But not expected to last very long. Because there was an abundance of them, the idea, was to simply put the gun on a new one, when they wore out. Instead of rebuilding an over strained, to ruin, engine. Also, they had to stop the car, and the gunners had to get out, to shoot. Only a hundred or two were in the main force. But a few that had to get out of their cars, and hopefully take a better aim, were considered a good thing.

The force had to move at marching speed, because of all the infantry. The only supply support they had, was 200 more 4 cylinder cars, half of which pulled small, once U-Haul trailers. Loaded with water bottles, fuel, food, and equipment too heavy to easily carry. But being typical Chinese infantry, they could cover a lot of ground in a day's time, compared to any other nation's infantry. Julius Caesar's army of Gaul, had nothing on them.

Daniel Conley was far from what heroes are usually made of. And he was barely a 16 year old kid. Yet, he became one of the, later to be, New American States greatest heroes. He was already much better known by his a.k.a. "Redbeard". Because of his long red hair, and a thin wispy, beard and moustache, that was only a teenage would sport. ...

Daniel was the leader of an Arizona militia, called the "The Wolverines". The name, of course, was copied from that old movie "Red Dawn". The reason he was the leader was, he made the deal with the Texas Military Liaison. He was a big, strapping, lad, with a knack for making people think he was smarter than he is. It was no coincidence, that no Wolverine members were over 17 years old. And any over 16 years old, were dumb or subservient personality types. Although there were only around 85 members in camp. The militia was listed, on paper, for the max authorized for them, 200. It was no coincidence, that over half the members were female.

They were currently camped about 2 miles west of Reno. Just a mile South of the zero maintained interstate 80 to California. The wide double road. The road was clear enough, but in poor repair. The Texans bought, or supplied, just about anything a militia could want. Food, ammo, a limited supply of petro, rifles, 2 belt loading machine guns, 2 anti air shoulder rocket launchers, a company car, you name it. They also entrusted Redbread with 4 doubloons per (listed) member, and a 10 doubloon bonus, every month. (Few of them were actually distributed to his troops.)

Doubloons were one of those currencies that were more valuable outside of its country. Because it was very stable. And they bought things in Texas, that were not available in Nevada. Such as fuel. In fact, they were more horded, than circulated.

(Federation Loyalists, was the name the warlord faction came up with for themselves. It was only lip service to the old fed government, and the newbies that actually joined the feds. In fact, about half the top warlords seemed to have vague plans, for a vaguely distant future, of replacing the feds with his, or her, own "superior" and "benevolent" leadership.)

The Texans boldly assumed no treachery from the Confederacy, the Federated Loyalist, nor the feds. And they sent nearly all of their military west. As soon as they could semi-organize it. The motto of the day, was "Get going! And get your act together on the way." Not many days later, the rest of the U.S.A. military sent troops into Arizona. But only token forces, at first. Each zero trusting the other. They sent at most 75% of their troops, and only gradually.

The motley collection of U.S.A. forces were soon gathering in Globe Arizona. It was almost a logistics disaster. The large majority of the troops missed more meals than not. And those they got, were usually pretty meager. (Don't do that to an American army for very long!) They were constantly debating, and bickering, which vehicles would get how much fuel, when it was serious military need, for them to actually crank up and move. Fortunately, pretty soon the U.S.A. got it into their heads to send less troops and vehicles, and more fuel and food. Excess troops were sent to Clifton (which wasn't named after me). And put troops to work building rafts, for a possible counter attack, down the Gila River.

The Chinese probably had hoped that the U.S.A. would not be able to defend Arizona so well. But they were still confident. In fact, they were happy that the U.S.A. was gathering for one desperate battle, that would decide who wins the war.

By the time Globe was looking less like a bedlam. The Chinese had secured and supplied Phoenix for their main forward base, and supply center. And were marching on Globe. Estimates of how many armored gun cars led the Chinese parade, varied wildly. But there were probably at least 12,000. The U.S.A. decided that a preemptive counter attack was the best defense. Little had been done to fortify Globe. And the terrain, was pretty open. Lead scouts of the Chinese, were with in 5 miles, when the U.S.A. sallied forth.

Nearly 1000 main battle tanks spread out to meet the Chinese armored gun cars. The whole U.S.A. couldn't keep that even that many tanks fueled for battle, for more than a few months. 800 and some change were sent (and very little else on the ground) by the feds. 105 were sent by Texas. The Confederacy and the Federated Loyalist contributed 3 or 4 dozen. The feds had more, but ammo was scarce, and not being produced. And the more sent, the less fuel would be there. The Chinese 110 mm. guns could destroy any tank they hit, more hits than not. And after shattering away ceramic/steel/composite armor, destroying the tank became even more likely. But the tanks could destroy the armored cars easier at 4000 meters, than the armored cars could destroy tanks at point blank range.

The tanks opened up, at what was estimated to be 6000 meters. Long, but not extreme range. (3.73 miles away!) About one fourth of the shots hit, and most of those destroyed an armored car. At that rate, the tanks would run out of ammo, before the Chinese ran out of armored cars. But they weren't going to spare anything, needed to win this battle. Seldom did a hit do spectacular looking damage. Except the occasional gas tank or ammo explosion. But when the black exploded dust cloud cleared, there was a wreck. Added to the diesel fumes from the beginning. Was burning fuel, with a taint of cordite. The only thing noisier than the constant tank guns, was the explosions. But not by much. It made the craziest thunderstorm, seem serene.

Maybe, the section of munitions plant that was now supposed to be making tank gun shells, was actually doing that. Perhaps, there were even shells on the way.

None of the armored cars tried to close the distance to their optimal, for this battle, 2000 or less meters. The only armored cars that shot back, were those with still a gun and crew, but no engine, wheels etc. At this range, they had to aim the cannon at an almost 45 degree angle, to reach the tanks. And it was woefully inaccurate. Even a perfect aim, had a one in 50 chance to hit. And as widely spaced as the tanks were, even less chance to hit one they weren't aiming at. So the Chinese officers didn't blame the car crews much, who quickly learned to abandon car, and run like hell, after firing only one shoot. The other cars, wheeled about, and retreated, orderly enough. Leaving nearly 1000 wreaks on the field.

But the Chinese had planned for this. The dozen or so VTOLs cruising the Chinese side of the battlefield, quickly became a much larger swarm. And swarmed the tanks. A non-stop rain of anti-tank missiles were launched. They were crude, but effective enough, when they hit. Which happened occasionally. In less than a minute, over 200 tanks were destroyed, main gun destroyed, or tracks broken. The ground troops returned some spectacular weapons fire. The 50 cal. machine guns scored a pathetic few kills and disables. And made quite a few less disabling bullet holes too. And in general, they kept the VTOLs high and nervous, hitting a lot less than they would have. Short range rocket fire made most of the kills. Large vehicle mounted Gatling guns did near as well. Especially within a 1000 meters. Even confederacy armored boxes mounted on cars, sporting 2 shoulder launched missile men, did surprisingly well. But VTOLs' Gatling guns did more than equal damage to the anti-air troops. The U.S.A. probably destroyed or disabled around 500 VTOLs. But more kept coming. Or would have, except:

The U.S.A. air force pounced! 400 and a dozen or two, the remnants of the fed air force, the best fighting planes in the world. Texas supplied an even 200 more. The Confederacy and the Federated Loyalists supplied about that many. Although the non-fed planes were mostly seriously inferior. Not that much more than 2/3rds of the fed air force were fighters, or fighter-bombers (ground attack), planes which were best for this battle. Everyone scrounged what they had, and sent them. The feds even slapped some 50 caliber machine guns on two C-173s, like they were WWII Flying Fortresses, but less, because the guns were aimed out windows and doorways, not cupolas.

Less than 30 seconds after the first VTOL loosed its first antitank rocket. 800 or so aircraft dived from behind the clouds, and flew thru the Chinese air force. First loosing missiles. Then Gatling guns and machine guns.

Over 900 VTOLs were destroyed. Or at least shot out of the air. The U.S.A. lost less than a dozen. And about half of those were lost in accidental collisions. Including one machine gun toting C-173 troop carrier (without troops)

Then the Chinese realized they couldn't destroy tanks, and defend themselves very well. As the VTOLs loaded with antitank missiles, were replaced with VTOLs loaded with air-to-air missiles, the fight was a lot more even. In fact, anytime the Chinese could fight with more than one to one, they did fairly well.

No more wild charges. The battle was, now, almost chess like, move and counter move. The tanks followed armored cars. But the armored cars were too fast. And stopping the tank still, for a decent shot, would add even more range. After about a 10 kilometer pursuit, the tanks began to encounter Chinese infantry. Everywhere there was decent cover. With an abundance of shoulder rocket launchers, the Chinese soldiers were far from ducks in a shooting gallery. And they numbered 1,250,000, ready to maneuver on the flanks, or reinforce the forward troops. The frag and high-explosive-plastic gun shells, that are best vs. infantry, were few among the tanks. The Chinese had thousands of 82 mm. mortars. After a few skirmishes. With the tanks shooting a couple of shots apiece, from well beyond shoulder launched rocket range. And killing less than 2 enemy soldiers a shell. A rain of mortar shells hammered the tanks. Dozens of hits. But no tanks disabled or destroyed. Periscope, antenna and other odd damage, that lessened a tank's effectiveness, until repaired. But it might have been worse! The tanks retreated.

The remaining C-173 charged thru a flock of VTOLs, machine guns blazing, scattering them like a bull would scatter wolves. It shot one down. It took 3 missile hits. If not for the armor that was added with the machine guns, any of those hits would have destroyed it. The pilot barely got it back and landed. After the additional damage of the landing, it was deemed not worth repairing. The two C-173s would have had some good strategic uses. This proved that modifying a C-173 for air battles, is a poor use.

The U.S.A. ground troops were digging in to a strong defense. With tanks 2000 meters back. And well protected by antiair weapons. The Chinese ground troops waited too. This battle would be decided by the air forces.

It was looking like the U.S.A. would run out of aircraft, before the Chinese. But other things decided the battle. That went on thru the night, and nearly to noon the next day. The U.S.A. air force practically ran out of ammo. And nearly out of fuel. They relocated to El Paso. 372 fit or repairable aircraft. The ammo sitz for the aircraft was about as bad, as for the tanks. They had shot up more ammo in this one battle, that they could manufacture in 30 days.

The VTOLs were almost out of fuel themselves. They could fly an average of another half hour. And pound the U.S.A. ground troops. And at great losses, destroy the U.S.A. tanks, from the air. But even then, against the dug in troops, the armored cars and mortars would not be enough, without an infantry assault. The U.S.A. had barely 200,000 soldiers. And a much lower percentage of shoulder rocket launchers. However, the U.S.A. rifles and machine guns would take a heavy toll. It the U.S.A. troops continued to fight tough, it would be a Pyrrhic victory. The Chinese decided to wait until more fuel arrived. Which should be less than a week. And they spend days hammering the U.S.A. troops from the air, first.

For a while the U.S.A.s awaited for the attack that never came. Before their aircraft left. They already set up a thin 10,000 men line of defense, 1000 meters behind the tanks. With 10 M-61 belt loading machine guns. Plenty, to slow down the Chinese infantry, to allow a retreat, instead of a rout and massacre. Once they realized the attack wasn't coming, they retreated. To Tucson would have left Texas vulnerable. And the army vulnerable to any Mexican treachery. So, the army went to El Paso, too.

20,000 mobile troops separated, and went to Albuquerque New Mexico. The Chinese would not take New Mexico without a fight, and a costly guerilla war. (Tanks were not considered "mobile troops". It took way too much fuel, to manage that. In fact, the U.S.A. tried to haul them on flat bed truck, whenever practical.)

When he finally heard about the Chinese offensive. A fed submarine commander decided to raid the China to California convoys. It was a little like "The Hunt For Red October" novel. But with a tragic ending. Even so, for over a month, the Chinese America fuel situation got even worse. Their main army stayed in Phoenix. (All the other surviving U.S. subs, had officially, or unofficially, joined the mighty Japanese Imperial Navy.) By the time the Chinese were rolling again. The U.S.A. forces had recovered, and reinforced. And had serious hopes of holding New Mexico. And would begin to, at least, take an air war and a guerilla war back into Arizona.

GUERILLAS AND CHIMPS

Northern California was only nominally under Chinese control. They kowtowed in exchange for peace, little interference, and only small taxes. Although the Chinese were gaining popularity, because of reasonable management. (They wisely decided to behave as if they had signed the Geneva and Hague Conventions. Including, forgoing the Asiatic military tradition, of raping the vanquished.)

Thru our connections, and the C.R.A.'s, we had pretty good info, on the northern California Chinese doings. We knew that the Chinese foot troops, along with their baggage etc. vehicles, made around 50 kilometers average, a little over 30 miles, on fairly flat, or paved ground. So, we could pretty well guess where they'd camp. So, we had a small chimp guerilla force waiting for them, 100 miles across the old California state line. The further away we met them, the more likely we'd get a second or 3rd chance.

As was the most likely odds, we guessed right the first time.

The Chinese camped out near the road. 3 touching close hills. And a lot of loose rock. A snowmelt from a mountain, gave the camp fresh drinking water. Easy to defend. The ground near the hills was very rough for non-4 wheel drive vehicles. So, the vehicles were in a well guarded parking area, nearer to the road. 100 infantry, and the drivers and crews, were camped near the vehicles. 10 at a time, patrolled around the vehicles.

What looked like just a brush pile, that floodwater had deposited, was actually deeper. Including a small puddle, that was about a foot at its deepest. Most of the brush, authentic driftwood, from other ravines, had been added. There was not much more than minimum room, for 20 soldier chimps, and their 4 JC breed handlers. Our chimps had been taught the knack for erasing tracks, without making it look like tracks had been erased. Luckily, no one gathered this brush, for firewood.

We had 4 levels of intelligence there. Or 5 or 6, if you count the chimp soldiers as 2 or 3 levels. The one smartest, was well below human mid average intelligence. But like the gangs in the projects, mentally "challenged" at birth, or by brain damage, usually from drugs. They usually muddle thru. They had a lot of training, and even some education, to do these sort of tasks.

Our chimp farm chimps would not have been good for this project. They would not have handled the boredom. The soldier chimps did fine. They were rigorously trained to discipline. So did the JC chimps we chose. They knew the reasons were important. And toughed it out. And the leader, Kevin, was even capable of some creative thinking. But, all that waiting was still a lot worse on the chimps, than it would be for hoomies.

12:00 midnight, by the digital watches, several of the chimps had. They emerged from their hiding place. The hoomies were camped out all over the 3 hills. Uh Oh! The detonators was in the middle of the hoomies' parking area. A complication. But the parking lot was the second objective, anyway.

These chimps carried the usual small backpacks. Civilian version M-16s, with bipods attached, and pistol gripped stocks. And shortswords with sheaths, on a utility belt, with a lot of cargo pockets. They also wore, designed for chimps, Kevlar, bulletproof vests[19]. Those were made

---

[19] There was also a type of armor, called scale mail. It had only some similarities to the, not very successful, medieval armor, by the same name. It was popular, among Texans rich enough to afford it, elite Texan motorized infantry. And a chimp version was popular among the more elite JC breed chimps. …

They were made of football type armor type plastic. Over that, was the 9mm. proof Kevlar. Under it was well done, shock absorbing, rubber padding. And over the Kevlar was steel plate scales. Sewn from factory Kevlar sheets, in a cottage industry. Not up to "specs" of the old factories, and mostly hand sewn. But that rarely made a difference. They were thin etc. That wouldn't stop anything faster than 9 mm. pistol bullets. But they'd take a lot of power out of any hand held firearm. Especially

---

on thin, synthetic, leather. That layer alone, was enough, to strip the jackets off of M-16/.223 hardball rounds. Leaving the small inner hard ball moving at b.b. gun speeds. It had similar style nazi style helmets. The visors to those were questionable. But could be flipped up, out of the way. Using a visor, it wasn't easy to see except, straight ahead, tunnel vision. The eye protector, wasn't 100% transparent, and would only stop .38 bullets. (Just one with cracks. Not even 9 mms.) And separate lace on neck, thigh and shim protectors. ...

An even 100 were given to us, as a return favor, and a disguised sales promotion. (Chimps with money, will buy anything. ☺) But even though they looked really snazzy, in "subdued black". They had very scant practical use. True, they were proof against all manner of rifle fire. And the very best armor available for melee combat. But only the feds considered chimp troops not too valuable, to use for front line combat. (And the feds didn't like us any more. ☺) That armor was too much encumbrance for guerillas etc. The only practical use we could see for it, was for an assassin, who wasn't planning to live thru it. ...

But we did special order 50 roman style curved, rectangular shields. Made out of the same stuff. But we had them modify it, to a "target shield" grip. That is, a center handle, so you could move it deftly. (Without 2 years of legionnaire training.) The Texans liked it. Soon, they be cranking them out, for their own troops.

military type M-!6 ammo. The difference, could make a lot of difference. ...

Kevlar helmets were available. But these guys preferred the cottage industry made "aviator" helmets, complete with goggles. They gave status to the owners, among chimps. And chimps were aware how cool, and dashing, those helmets made chimps appear, to hoomies.

A single chimp observed the parking area, from a slightly higher vantage point. After an hour, they were confident in the hoomies regular, enough, patrol patterns. It was a quarter moon, and partially cloudy. Too much light, by chimp thinking. Actually, it was simple. Once a sentry walked by, there would be around 100 meters between him and the next one. The trick would be to cross their paths silently. Far enough behind the first, that a casual backward glance from him, wouldn't see the chimp. The rule of thumb would be, it you saw the next hoomy, as more than a small blurred blob. Then you needed to go back, or forward whichever way is the quickest.

A small "dry" runnel, that still had wet mud in it, led in the general direction, 7 or 8 meters from, a medicine ball sized boulder. About half the boulder was underground, leaving a half sphere exposed. Barely adequate concealment for a chimp. It was about 30 meters from one of the vehicles. Under the vehicle would be good concealment.

The first one to go, would be a JC chimp, Charlie. He was the second smartest. So, he was the best one, to scout out the vehicle park. And then he came back to give his report.

A little past 2:00 a.m. All chimps were in the parking area. One was left, at the first vehicle, a cargo car, in case someone picked up their trail.

About that time, a hoomy did notice the tracks, that he was sure were not there, when his watch started. He figured it was probably a pack of wild dogs. He trailed the tracks to the first vehicle. Well, there was a lot of mischief and damage, a pack of wild dogs could get into, in that parking lot. So he called up on his 2 way radio. At some point it was reported to someone, who was more suspicious. And who even decided that there was a possibility, that those were chimp tracks. A 10 man squad, to kill or drive off the wild dogs, or whatever, arrived. The sentry continued his rounds. 3 of his fellows had already passed him.

The chimp on watch by that car, had been ready, had the sentry come any closer than in front of that car. The chimp would have surely chopped the sentry's head off, with his shortsword.

Now when he saw a 10 man squad of riflemen start walking the same trail, he knew they were coming. He spread the warning in the quickest, quiet enough way. He scamper ran and gave a low volume version of the "enemies coming" hoots. And held up 10 fingers. By the time he warned the fourth one, the others had already warned the rest. Kevin gave a few changes in orders. They had planned to leave with 24 vehicles. But they'd be lucky to escape with their lives, even with the new plan.

The Chinese "hunting" squad was ready for a hunt, not a firefight. They were all bunched together, AK-49s in hand, but not particularly ready. A belt loading light machine gun, on an armored gun car, ripped into them. In about 5 seconds, and 50 or so rounds, all had fallen in a heap, dead or dying. That was the signal, for the rest of the show. (Actually, the agreed signal was, "As soon as anybody start shooting. …") 2 more machine guns opened up on the foot soldier camp near the vehicles. The 20 armored gun cars started cranking up. But some took 30 seconds more to crank up.

And the most spectacular thing of the whole operation. Charlie attached a 9 volt battery to a battery clip, in the detonator rig. Although there was a lot of voltage drop, due to the distance of the wires. There was still more than the 1.5 volts and miniscule amps, needed to detonate the explosives. 20 one kilo high explosives rocked the night, and lit up the sky. Slinging shrapnel all over the 3 hills. It seemed to the Chinese, that the small, high velocity, nails were everywhere.

Charlie was probably the first to fire off his 110 mm. cannon. He turned one of the near camp's tents into flying shrapnel. The orders were, shoot at whatever looks like the most fun. Which is a pretty good order to give chimps. Chimps are brave, relaxed and clever in battle, as all long as they're having fun. The cannons were spectacular, but didn't do much damage. They were loaded with HEAT[20] shells. There had been no time to fumble and reload them with better shells, v. infantry. After he fired off that shot. He switched to that armored car's light machine gun. And he was that driver's machine gunner, for the ride.

Once all the armored cars were cranked up and idling. The drivers fired the loaded shot, from their cannon. The shot was already aimed, so that was pretty quick. Except Charlie's driver, who simply drove off, and was in the lead.

It was amazing that the Chinese got over their shock, surprise and terror so soon. That they

fired off over 100 shoulder launched rockets. Which roared after the armored cars. Fortunately, the range was very long, and most of the hands on the launchers were shaky. So it wasn't all that amazing, that only 3 armored

---

[20]   H.E.A.T. (High Explosive Anti Tank) Shaped explosives, focusing the blast, to cut thru very thick steel. Designed to destroy tanks and armored cars. But it contained no shrapnel. And it's blast was directed in one very narrow direction. The shell itself, did turn into a few hunks of shrapnel.

cars were hit. Those chimps were counted as missing, presumed dead. We never heard from them again. The Chinese wouldn't dare pursue the chimps, with their cargo cars. Even though less than a dozen tires had been slashed. (When their exit became urgent, there was too much, more important, needing to be done.)

And there was no worry about the 3 VTOLs. Already, 3 chimps were learning to fly them, on their way back to Reno. The 3 Chinese pilots and 3 co-pilot gunners, would not know they were missing, until well after sunrise. Courtesy of 6 C.S.A. sex workers. They should have known, unless you are a "hunk", sex with pretty hoomy women is rarely, truly, free.

When I was a child ... But When I became a Man, I Put Away The Things of a Child.

Sunrise, the same day, if counting 12:01 midnight as the start of a new day, of the hit and run, on the Chinese expeditionary force. Redbeard's Camp.

7 chimps wandered into the Wolverines' camp, and to the front flap of Redbeard's large pup style tent, without being detected. They didn't have to bother with much stealth. Even a hoomy would have had no problem doing that.

Their leader, Redbread was sound asleep. Like most everyone else. The chimps' leader Kevin, slapped on the tent flap, a less noisy substitute, for knocking on a door. When the second time didn't produce results, he gestured to his lieutenant, Charlie, to do the same, to a tent next door. A vague several pointings, imparted the idea to keep doing it, until he found someone. 3rd try. A 15 year old or so, skinny male teenager, with moderate length brown hair; was fairly quick out of his tent, holding a coffee cup. His bored expression quickly turned into a Wow! Cool! expression. He ambled over to Redbeard's tent, opened the flap an inch, and yelled inside, an inch or two from the flap, "Heyeyeyey REDBREAD!!! The Chinese are coming!!! They're just over the ridge!!!"

About 3 seconds later, Redbeard, red hair flying, charged out of the tent snarling. The first thing from the tent, was a Texas made civilian M-16[21]. He was looking for someone to shoot. And he probably wasn't all that particular, whether it was Chinese or not. Charlie grabbed the rifle barrel near the muzzle, and lifted it in the air, so nobody would get hit, if it went off. At least, no one in the camp. Redbeard tried to twist and shake his rifle loose. But he could not. Meanwhile, the other chimps, except Kevin, started patting Redbeard on the back and shouilders, chattering soothingly. This had a negative effect. Not that Redbeard was a homicidal maniac. But he hated being woke up, and he hated looking bad in front of his "troops". But after 30 seconds, he calmed down enough to notice that Kevin had stopped scribbling, and was trying to hand him a slip of paper.

---

[21] You can tell by the five pointed star of both sides of the stock. Subdued off white.

Redbeard took the slip of paper, and read it. Scrawled over a blank spot was, "Chinese are coming. But not that close." Fortunately, it was legible enough. We never bothered trying to teach chimps cursive writing, so it was printed.

Then a pretty female teenager, wearing nothing but extra scanty pink panties, opened the tent, and stared at the chimps. Who too obviously weren't immune to her charms! And weren't wearing any clothes, themselves. Her hair was dark blondish, a very cute face. She probably wasn't much older than 15 years old, but an early bloomer. What she was missing in curves, she more that made up for, with her waist length hair, and teenaged cuteness. When she saw the teenaged boy gawking, and almost drooling. And he managed to spill some of his coffee, even though it was only about a quarter full. She turned pink in the face, started giggling, as she grabbed a blanket, and wrapped it around herself. Then thought better, and simply closed the tent flap. Still giggling.

The underneath message was; "Chinese are coming. They could be here as soon as 9:00 a.m. At least 1500. Too many to fight. Reno has already been warned. Any who care, are leaving. U.S.A. command wants you to head east about 100 kilometers. Then head to what used to be the Nevada-Arizona border. Await further orders, by a U.S.A. Major or higher." (Redbread was a captain. Quite an honor. Only a little over 10% of the new U.S.A., and Texan, forces were officers.)

Redbread tried gently to pull his rifle loose, again. After a nod from Kevin, Charlie let loose. Nobody died. ☺ (Hoomies get very upset, and irrational, when you take their guns away. Especially the military trained ones.)

Kevin fished out a second slip of paper, and unfolded it, obviously it had been pre-written, like the last note. It read; "How would you like to have 17 Chinese armored gun cars?! How bout 3 Chinese VTOLs?! And we have 3 chimps to teach you how to fly them. But they're still learning themselves. Hoomies very good drivers! Be honored! These are the first VTOLs ever captured. ... By the way. Fun and games are over. You recruit a full 200 soldiers, and try to keep that many." He held the note to the smaller, skinny, teenager, for a quick scan read, before he handed it to Redbeard. Before Redbeard's eyes focused on the paper, the teenager said "I want to fly a VTOL!" Redbread mumbled something about, "drag your [donkey] from a VTOL on a chain."

... This was bad news to Redbeard. More than even most adults, he was aware how crazy all this military madness was. But there was nothing really left for him to do, but go along with it. Jobs were scarce, and most of the very few available were hard physical work.

But soon he started enjoying it. And he was developing more and more talent as a guerilla leader. His army that left Reno, had slightly less females than males. And they tended to mostly pull their own weight. Except for Redbread's 3 young, pretty, and curvaceous, "wives". Although he now recruited some older women, few of the males were older than him, and none were a leadership challenge threat.

And he got better all the time. He became the great hoomy guerilla leader, Redbeard, that you can read about in hoomy history books.

Even so, the man never came close to living up to the legend. Redbeard's famous march to Albuquerque, with many diversions, and escapades between, didn't really kill very many Chinese, nor destroy nor capture, much Chinese supplies nor equipment. But the effect of their own vehicles attacking them from assorted unpredictable, surprise, northern directions, caused major confusion, panic, and useless deployment of a lot of Chinese troops. And it inspired a lot of copycats, looking for loot and glory, for themselves.

The Chinese had major problems stretching supply lines thru, and occupying so much. Thru chimp sympathizers, I republished some of my old revolutionary days how-to pamphlets. Including a superior to factory made, homebrew silencer design. And my famed "One

Shot Cannons".[22] Guerilla warfare and more guerilla warfare was becoming the order of the day.

They had to take Nevada, just to protect themselves from guerillas. But Nevada was so sparsely settled, that they only tried to control and tax Reno and Las Vegas. They continuously raided the rest, treating it as if a buffer zone.

---

[22] Those were basically just that. Powered by pipe bombs or high explosives. Use just once because the "barrel" pipe explodes, too. Limited to your imagination! Giant, super powered, shotguns could do titanic destruction. Guerillas could knock down buildings from over 100 meters off. By fuse or timer, they could blast an enemy camp, with thousands of very high velocity metal darts, long after the guerilla crept away. ... Guerilla warfare would never be the same.

THE MOST FAMOUS COUPLE IN THE WORLD

The afternoon, before the chimp raid on the Chinese expeditionary force to Nevada. Colonel Jackson called Hiro to his office. Which was a commandeered hotel room, in an abandoned hotel. After the greetings, which Hiro didn't much more than mumble to, with a stoney impassive face. Colonel Jackson went straight to the point. "The Chinese are marching on Reno. Around 2000 of them. I and my men have been ordered to leave for Denver Colorado. I am also ordered to order a platoon to stay behind. And under a peaceful white flag, deliver your rocket center to the Chinese. I see no reason why I should waste manpower deploying any of my men for that. So I am appointing that job to you, and your people. Well I have to go." he said, as he stood up, patted Hiro on the shoulder, and was walking towards the door, "My troops are ready. The sooner the better. Before some fool shoots me as a traitor, or deposes of me as commander. There's already been a lot of that sort of thing going on, lately.", as they vigorously shook hands a dozen or so seconds. "We will head east for a while. But soon we will go south, to join either the C.S.A. or Texas. Whichever we find first. Good Luck! I sure hope you have enough time. Bye." …

Hiro got over his total shock in a dozen or so seconds. And formed a tentative plan. Hiro was not near as unprepared as he might have been. He too, knew the Chinese were coming. And he was already preparing for a wild plan, to siege his rocket complex, and launch the moon rocket. It might have had as much as an even change to succeed. And if so, the hastily launched rocket would have had would have had about an even chance to succeed. But this was MUCH better.

Chuck, now man-in-the-moon Chuck, had married his contest chosen bride, a week after he landed, via satellite communications. His bride, Britney Monroe, now changed her name, yet one more time, to Eve Starwoman. Although she was very qualified, both in genes, intelligence. And thanks to crash training, as a fairly good space worker. Nor was she really a slut, by modern standards. Certainly not a sex worker. Receptionist and Spokes Model were her sort of jobs. But it was obvious that if Chuck chose her for her space worthy traits, they were certainly secondary. And she was just the, apparently, ditzy blonde, living on her looks, that Allison and her comrades hated.

In a desperate, very un-libish, attempt to get Chuck to change his mind. They informed Chuck she recently had an operation to restore her virginity. It had the opposite effect on Chuck. He thought it was a nice, thoughtful, bonus. Eve was wroth with Allison and her comrades. For ruining her surprise, and thoroughly embarrassing her in the world public. They ruined their chance of bringing her into the neutral side, of their power struggle. And certainly what little chance, that she'd join them.

The payload was considered 75% to 90% wasted, depending on who figured it; towards the long-term moon colony plans. But it would give Chuck and Eve a very good chance to survive, into old age. … 4 more doors and frames. 800 kilos of bottled air, including bottle weight. Eve and a VERY small wardrobe. 2 rabbits. 2 chickens. Mushroom culture. A large can of worms. A sophisticated, but small, hydroponics set up. More tools and gadgets. A very large ROM info library. 500 kilos of dehydrated, dried, very low water content, food, and animal feed, soy protein, and vitamin and mineral pills.

And in case of wore case: There were an even 1000 sperm samples, to provide gene diversity, for the next generation.

The only frivolous item, was a 2 kilo wedding cake.

The Chinese expedition took over 25% killed and wounded, from the chimp raid. They used most of their cargo vehicles to carry wounded back to California. It would be a day before those vehicles returned. After a half day of burials and ceremonies, the Chinese marched on. The soldiers were loaded with supplies and equipment, that was not on the returning vehicles. So that day's progress was little. As Reno came into sight, they saw the rocket launch.

5 minutes later, Hiro was heading east, with plans to head south to Texas, after they reached Albuquerque. But unlike Redbread, Hiro planned the safest, more northerly, route. And he was ready to modify the route, even a lot, to stay safest. The centerpieces of Hiro's convoy was 3 dump trucks. The rest was an assortment of over 60 family and economy cars. One of the dump trucks, was in ways, a spare. It carried fuel, water, food and personal possessions that would have over loaded the smaller vehicles. But if a dump truck had broken down, beyond repair, a lot of hard decisions would have to be made. The other 2 dump trucks were treasure trucks. Full of an amazing variety of low bulk, high (fed) Hour per kilo value, trade goods. Many tools, and gadgets, rich folks clothes, quite a few duffle bags full of assorted ammo, and even 100 kilos of gold, that was now rising rapidly in value. And who knows what else. (Fuel was still very valuable. But one didn't carry fuel to Texas.)

He was accompanied by over a hundred armed and dangerous retainers. His trusted and loyal retainers, a few friends, and his space program folks, who had stood by him, during his many set backs and disasters, and a few victories. (Allison Rand and her comrades could be counted as that. But they were still living in her Colorado mansion. Colorado had become a refugee camp, for ex-rich folks, and a small sprinkling of still rich folks. Hiro, wisely, didn't inform Allison of his plans.)

The convoy was cruising about the max speed of the Chinese cargo cars, unless they unloaded. About the same max speed for any 4 cylinder armored cars, if they still had any. Not that the Chinese had any intent of doing anything more than occupying Reno, and dabble at anti-guerilla warfare, for at least a month. The convoy would be very safe. They looked like a typical poor, but larger and better armed that usual, refugees. That were already beginning to migrate from Nevada. Also inside each dump truck, was an M-60 design belt loading machine gun, ready to be revealed in a few seconds. And a gunner was always in the dump trucks, 24/7. A nasty surprise for any bandits etc.

Hiro gave up on his space program. It was all in the hands of Chuck and Eve, now. Hiro had done his best. And did amazingly well. Unlike the vast majority of this planet, Hiro had a lot of confidence in Chuck and Eve.

Of course. Eve made it. Although she didn't quite match Chuck's moon landing record. She was some proof of the superiority (reflexes) of women drivers. Even in space ships. Hers landed 283 meters from Chuck's. Bordering an often sunlit area, hers would be the "out building" to the farm land".

GOVERNMENT BY THE GOVERNMENTS AND FOR THE GOVERNMENTS

The Chinese were, of course, primarily interested in conquest at a profit. They had no wish to maintain a constant expense of military resources, at little or no profit. Especially in the increasingly turbulent world sitz. And reviving a Russian Empire. And the vast uprising, in guerilla warfare, was very determined, and smarter and better organized than any time in history. And magnified by modern technology. (The roman legionnaire's worst fear from guerillas was arrows, poison in the food and cup, and daggers in the dark. We had plenty of that, too. But we also had semi-auto rifles and better. And shrapnel bombs, and many other varieties.)

So. The Chinese were, now, very willing to negotiate with the feds. Keeping California sounded pretty good. And especially if they could get some or all of Arizona, and maybe Reno and Las Vegas, too. The feds were ready to deal. Including on all of those points, if they, directly to them only, were paid some generous foreign aid, and official Chinese recognition, as the overlord government of U.S.A. The feds still had their nuke missiles, mostly functional. And the Chinese could of course, deliver nukes and other "NBC", via their aircraft. But so far, since WWII, that just wasn't done. They were just the ultimate spoiled sport bargaining chip, of last resort.

But Texas, the Confederacy, and the Federated "Loyalists", had tasted blood. They would settle for no less, than the liberation of all the 48 U.S.A. states. Fed treachery became more and more apparent. It came to the point, that the majority of the powers that be, among the Confederacy and Federated Loyalists, were about to declare war on the feds.

The Chimp Nation was more reasonable. Give us a few hundred square miles of fertile land, our possessions, peace and trade, and we'd be happy. Who really cares what the hoomies do to each other?! Until we overpopulate that land. ☺ But our mutual hatred with the feds, was long standing.

Armies Are Always Trained to Fight The Last War

I got a (phone) e-mail from JC. "Everyone else wants to go to war against the Feds. They want your personal opinion. And to know how much support we will give them." "Do whatever it takes, to stop that stoopidity. Now we have the advantage over the Chinese. The Feds are so scattered, that Fed power could be crushed within a month. But by that time, we can expect so much disruption. That the balance of power v. the Chinese would shift. And without the feds pretending to be the overlords, the other 2 factions will be squabbling with each other. Which in turn, will cause squabbling within the factions. A lot more than there already is. … Tell them I said 'We'll handle it ourselves.'" "How are we going to do THAT?!" "Tell them I didn't tell you anything. And don't tellthemnothing! And when you know something, tell them, I told you don't tellthemnothing(!) About every 10th U.S.A. soldier is, at least an amateur spy for some side or the other." "Right!

But how are we going to do it? "I don't trust these e-phones to be secure anymore. So, I'll send you a letter to send copies of to any, and all, news media. And to a few other folks. While you're waiting: Gather, keep on hand and rested, the best and most versatile assassin talent we have, among the expendables, and semi-expendables. At least 20 JC chimps and at least 20 soldier chimps. Be prepared to keep that many, in constant stockpile. This is going to be our new "art of war". ...

"A main weakness of hoomies, is their need of leaders. The vast majority are not much better than sheep. You can be pretty sure, if you kill #1 and #2. Then #3 will be more reasonable. You can literally control nations, and even individual armies, by killing those that are most unfriendly to you. Even with hoomies, by the 1950's, this should have been the state of the art of war. But rich hoomies don't wage war to knock each other off. They war to kill working folks hoomies, and steal territory from each other. Even so. You see a few glimmers of this. The old U.S.A. mafia, and the Kennedy assassination, for instance. And if you believe the old Japanese ninja, mostly myths. The only difference between when we slapped Space Donkeys around and now. Is the scale. And waiting a week to hear from them. ...

"'Dune', by Frank Herbert, should have given you a pretty good feel for this. Note the "War of Assassins" and "Canly" references. Oh! I bet you never got around to reading "Dune", we've been too busy. No matter. "Dune" is a great classic. But better for this, would be the "ShadowRun" series. I doubt if many paper copies are still available. But the complete set, should be on the Internet. Lots of details. And some of the details can be applied. Also, it will give you the idea of what hoomie social organization will change to, when we loose this art of war, as the state of the art. ... Anyway! When you get the message. Do what it takes, to make this plan work. And make any changes you think smart. Consider it like football. I am handing the ball off to you, to make a touchdown. The messenger will leave within an hour of this message. Enjoy! (I know you will!)☺

<u>The letter.</u> To Prez Northwitch, a.k.a. Prez Elmer Fudd. We are giving you one last chance, to behave like a reasonable sentient being. And negotiate a peace settlement with us. Please name a neutral place and time, within 7 days of this date.

We have reason to believe, that the following people will die: [20 names and titles] ... "Please note that we expect them all to die, the next day after this letter's post mark. In case you have any doubts about our magic powers of divination. ☺

We regret the need to give you a demonstration of our power. Be aware that we very avoid killing working folks. Nor even soldiers. Who are only fighting for their land and people. However misguided they may, or may not, happen to be. We only want perpetrators of evil to die.

I hope you answer and agree. We monitor most of the major television stations, and U.S.A. Today. I hope you see fit to answer in time. I think that would be a lot better. In any case, we are always ready to negotiate. We will never again disturb your harmony, with any death predictions. Cliff Atreides, Caesar, The Chimp Nation

We listed 20 people. 12 letters were sent to newspapers and TV. stations. 1 letter to Prez Northwitch, noted on all the other letters we sent. The fed post office was mostly dysfunctional. Really, not much use for it. But some important government officials, and some rich folks, just liked the idea and feel of a "real" letter. So dozens of the largest non-anthraxed cities did still have it, even after the anthrax. And those were linked together. 2 or 3 dozen more still had it, but only post office to post office. (Retrieve your own mail.) As happened, Prez Northwitch got his first copies from others we sent to.

We missed 2 targets, 2 chimp assassins were killed, including one who missed, actually didn't get in shortsword range. One killed his target, but was captured. He was a soldier chimp, who took his cyanide tablet, from the necklace medallion and suicided. Before they could take it from him. That kept them from "hard ball" "tactical" interrogating him. Actually we thought that was pretty good. To show that chimps can get just as fanatic as any beings. We only used one shrapnel bomb. Just to remind them. That we are very good with bombs. Besides that, some of the rest of the hits were harder than necessary. After all, this was entirely a sheer demonstration of power. I think 3 hits are worth mentioning.

One. Air Force General "Bomber" Harrison of Omaha. He was in command of the mostly mothballed B-54 nuke bombers. He often threatened, quite seriously, to nuke cities in the 48 U.S.A. states. And especially China, Hawaii and Alaska. It was scary to anyone in the U.S.A.; that the only person who could control him, was his friend, and fellow psycho, Prez Northwitch. Of course, that tended to worry everyone else in the world, too.

Large military bases are notoriously easy to sneak into. If you're a chimp, the wilderness areas they keep for training etc., make them even easier. No security on personnel housing, beyond the usual cheap locks. Even General Harrison didn't bother with a home security system. Nobody known to reside on a military base, could get by with a known crime, if the military chose to investigate enough.

Someone, probably a teenager, broke into General Harrison's bathroom window. And stole his Play Station VII, out of his living room, and left out of the broken window. It was thought that General Harrison died of a heart attack, a few hours later, soon after he got home. It was guessed that the anger-stress of the break in, theft, caused it.

Until two hours after the fed military command read a copy of my letter. A better (competent) autopsy was done. It was found that he died of p. cyanide poisoning. And traces of it found partially digested medicine capsule, that was found in his stomach. Sure enough, his heart medicine capsules had been replaced with identical capsules, containing p. cyanide. … We could have use something that wouldn't have showed up in an autopsy. Or just one pill in the bottle, if we were in no hurry. But, we WANTED credit.

Soon after, all U.S.A. military high commands, of every faction, scoured the market, for any, and all, existing security electronics.

Two. Northwitch's shoeshine man. Who was often called to the White House, to shine Northwitch's shoes. He hung out most days, shining shoes about a hundred meters down the street. He was likely the last person in the U.S.A. to shine other people's shoes for a living. We very avoided killing working folks. But we knew the "shoeshine" was really a fed agent. Who carried orders from Northwitch to generals and agents. Less and less, Northwitch trusted his own staff, cabinet and generals. Paranoia tends to be a self fulfilling prophesy.

The two Secret Service men that were sent to fetch the "shoeshine", found him laying face down, in the gutter. Dead from a slit throat. The blood stopped flowing into the drain. The G-men were the first to bother reporting the crime.

As we hoped this hit upset Northwitch the most.

Three. Again in Washington DC. A 4 cylinder nondescript, blue, Toyota pulled up to the curve, in front of the Supreme Court Building. Out jumped 5 short, pudgy, bandy legged, clowns. In typical clown suits, big round balls on the nose of their clown masks, funny hair, of 5 different impossible shades, and 2+ foot long shoes. They capered up the Supreme Court steps.

They all had guitar cases slung on their backs. One up front, also had a drum he was beating on. Without a whole lot of rhythm. The cheap drum sounded like it had seen better days. The driver was behind them. He also carried a giant, oversized, fake, cartoonish red colored, pistol. The type that you expect to squirt water, or some other sort of silliness. Then, a sheet of paper spreads our, with "Bang!" written on it.

The Supreme Court had seen a lot better days. In fact, it was just a relic left over from pre-anthrax days. Not only did nobody care about the fine points of fed law. Nobody really cared about fed law, period. Fed law had been made very simple. Just obey higher ranking feds. Even so, the same influence that got them the job, kept them the job. When the salaries were translated from dollars to Hours, they lost a lot. But they still made more than most everybody else. For commenting on and deciding a whole lot, about very little. At a stately, sedate, pace. Really, not all that much different from what they had been doing before the anthrax. They were down to one clerk and one secretary apiece. The only visible security they had, was the old man manning the metal detector, in front of the door. (Because none had much influence with Prez Northwitch, himself.) In keeping with the wild new times, besides his old service revolver, he had an M-16 assault rifle. But it was strapped onto his back.

He stood up, and smiled, "Does anybody in there know you're coming?" Then the driver emerged from the others, as they split in two, going around the metal detector. The driver clown pointed his funny-pistol at the guard, and fired. A loud metallic <Thunk!>, and a metal bolt was sticking out of the guard's forehead. The guard did a sort of spastic, jittering, dance, as and after he fell. By now, the 4 clowns drew pistol grip civilian M-16s out of their guitar cases. Then they charged thru the front door shooting, at anything alive. Fortunately, for us, the building very muffled the shots.

The driver realized that there was nothing he could do, to increase the mission's success chances. In fact, the mission was now an almost certain success. He was a JC breed chimp, not expendable cannon fodder. So, he dragged the guard into a shadowy corner. Then calmly capered back to his car. He was soon driving away, slow and lawfully. If any of the others made it to the rendezvous point, he would very gladly drive them south, back into Confederacy territory. He was going that way himself.

The idea was for them to kill as few people as possible, besides the 9 Supreme Court Justices. But these guys' hoomy recognition skills just weren't up to that. They might have been able to spare the females. But one of the Justices was female. The place ended up looking like a slaughterhouse. Blood spreading and clotting on most places. And that nice slaughterhouse aroma, too. In war, bad things happen, often for stupid reasons.

There were 9 bodyguards, one for each of the justices, with 12 gauge pump shotguns, and billy clubs. 4 bodyguards and 4 justices, made it to 5 judges chambers, and locked the doors. The rest died in the main lobby and offices. One clown took a shotgun blast to the chest. But he barely noticed it. His suit was holed, and was leaking Styrofoam from a pillow.

Now the clowns were placing explosive rectangular grenades next to the doors. Turning a timer switch. And jumped back into the middle of the Courtroom. <BOOM! BOOM! BOOM!> While one clown overwatched with his rifle. Then they threw frag grenades, thru the splintered and barely together doors. Another less together <BOOM! BOOM! BOOM!> Realizing what was going on, a body guard charged out of his judge's chambers, and surprised a chimp that held, but not aimed, his rifle one handed, while setting the high explosive grenade. A shotgun blast hit the chimp in the chest, ripping away costume and pillow pieces. A second blast ripped away most of the rest from his chest area, and quite a few scale "mail" discs. But zero penetration into the rest of the vest. The shotgun blasted at the chimp's head, but the chimp ducked the aim, and all the pellets missed. The overwatch chimp finally got a clear shot, and plinked 8 shots into the hoomy bodyguard. And another thru his head, as he laid still on the marble floor.

While that was going on, the de-costumed chimp noticed that his timer was dangerously short. He threw it thru the 4 inch opened door. A big <Whump!>, and the door flew wide open. That chimp charged in, in the smoke, and shot twice at obscured inanimate objects. And found the female Justice lying on the nice rugged floor, barely conscious, and completely stunned. He shot her thru the head, which exploded a fist size hole, on the other side of her head. And he scampered out of the room to join the others.

It was soon over, a frag grenade for each of the unlocked chambers. Just to make sure. The last locked door fell to the high explosive grenade, backed up with the frag grenade, trick. All Justices not already shot in the head, were. They smashed open the drum. And then divided up, the extra clips of ammo, and some more frag grenades, that were inside. And the chimp clowns bolted out the front door.

As they ran down the steps. 2 police patrol cars pulled up at the curve, screeching to a jumping stop. The chips shot first, 3 rounds apiece. None of the 3 cops per car were hit. But it was close. Glass flying everywhere. One had managed to get out of the car, on the far side. He crouched down out of sight. And then down on the pavement, looking under the car, for a foot or ankle to shoot at. The other cops hid down, behind the imperfect cover of the thin, light, sheet metal doors. The chimps shot slower, and as well aimed as running would allow. At places they thought a hoomy might be. The one with most of his costume shot off, leaped on top of that car's roof. And as he leaped off the car, he shot 3 shots, one handed, into the hoomy aiming his M-16 under the car. A second later, a frag grenade apiece landed inside each car. <Whoom! Whoom!>. And miraculously, one, gas tank DID manage to catch fire. And the flames slowly consumed most of the car. The lead chimp peeled off his ruined costume, displaying the scale mail armor. That was also missing some scales.

And the chimps ran on, into the closest housing project. More shooting and liberal overuse of frag grenades, and the chimps made it out of the city. And eventually to the rendezvous place.

Why didn't we kill Prez Northwitch?! One. He was the best saboteur of the fed cause. Two. A great scapegoat, for when it was in our interests, to unite the hoomies. Three. Someone else would get around to killing him for us. Four. We wanted his established "leadership" ☺ to answer to us. Five. Unless we used bombs, his super security would have been too risky to the chimp assassins. Six. We were considering, taking him out, if he did not negotiate. But only after we sent negotiation missives, to #1 and #2 in line.

DIPLOMACY IS OFTEN A CONTINUATION OF WAR, BY OTHER MEANS.

The upper level feds were in terror. Even so, they slow walked us 6½ days, trying to prove they were tough. To me, it was just showing weakness. I was quite prepared to sling at them, 2 dozen or so assassins a week. (Heck! In the Chimp Nation, they grow on trees. ☺) Then, they slow walked us, for yet another 2 weeks. Demanding meeting places, that were far from neutral. Finally, they did offer a neutral place. South of Wichita Kansas. Just north of the Texas protectorate of Oklahoma. Texas was pretty friendly with chimps, these days. But. They insisted that we meet them inside their mobile Command Center van. Northwitch wouldn't be there in person. But by video and audio. And a general would be there in person. He would have 8 soldiers. There would be 6 of us, counting JC. They would have guns, we would not. It looked like possible treachery. But we took those thoughts as over-caution, and an attempt to intimidate us, at the negotiation table.

Treachery would have been foolish. This was big world news.

Then another fed spin. They insisted that I show up, too. JC arranged ATV travel for me, all the way to I-10. From there, I was carried by a Confederate armor clad car. Now, treachery COULD accomplish something. The Chimp Nation would be a lot weaker, if it lost both me and JC. But we went for it. We were very contemptuous of fed troops close quarter fighting ability, anyway. We did get them to bring their van across the bridge, over the bordering creek.

The armor clad stopped at the Oklahoma – Kansas border. JC got in the car, with the 5 bodyguard chimps JC brought. They were all wearing Texas scale mail armor, with all the leg and arm accessories, and were carrying mail shields. And each had 2 shortswords in sheaths, attached to belts. They put the shields and helmets in the trunk. And hopped into the car. I decided it was time to don my armor, and did so as we drove on. That was a several minute chore, to do expertly. And sitting in a now crowded car, to took several more minutes. But there was still plenty of time.

I said to JC, who was sitting next to me, with his ever ready notebook and pen, "I think it's about time we made you the highest leader." <Why?> "If I'm not the supreme commander, I can get on with my life, not much different than any other millionaire or billionaire. The hoomies will get the idea that they need me, to negotiate with you. So, I should never be that much of an assassination target. But you, I'm sorry to say, will always be a big target, no matter what. You'll have to live like a like a South American, self-elected, dictator, anyway. Besides. You guys are worthy of your own Supreme Leader. And we need to show that to the world." <Makes sense to me. You're already the Chimp Nation's Ceasar. So, I'll call myself "Emperator".> "I think we should announce it, at this negotiation." …

There were a hundred fed riflemen 1000 meters back from the bridge. Our Texas escort, also 100 riflemen, was 1000 meters southish of the bridge. The Texas armor clad stopped at this invisible border. And we dismounted and walked forward. The fed Command Van was already crossing the bridge.

With our armor, shields and helmets, we looked more like medieval foot soldiers, than diplomats. Not being a chimp super-fighter, I would do best at semi-classic fencing. So in place of one short sword, I had a combat, not ceremonial, version of a U.S. cav saber.

2 soldiers, with M-16s in hand, and automatic pistols in holsters, were waiting for us, on either side of the van's back door, which was facing us. There was a small, roundish, speaker next to one. An appliance type insulated set of wires, led from the speaker, and was jacked into

the van. There was a small, seemed like probably bullet resistant, viewing slot in the back door. The soldier next to the speaker said "Leave your weapons, shields and helmets here. You can keep your armor on, if you are afraid. But no helmets. We want to see your faces when you speak. And it's too crowed for the shields." I replied "I don't think so. Maybe you should just drive this van to Dallas. There we can let the Texans worry about security." JC shook his head at me, and started scribbling. <Don't worry about it. I have it under control.> I should have backed away and left, and let JC handle the negotiations, if he still wanted to. But something in his expression made me think different.

They used metal detector, and x-ray wands on us. They inspected JC's pens very carefully. The rest of us got this unwanted attention. Which included taking our armor on and off. Which we insisted, would be one at a time. Whatever JC had, he got it past the detectors.

Suprisingly, via slow hydraulic, the van's door opened like a drawbridge. And it was a ramp into the command center. We walked up the ramp and entered. The command center was too cozy for this many. Pres Northwitch's smiling face, obviously live, was already on a big TV screen on the far wall. The van room was 5 meters long, 3 meters wide. Plenty of padded backed stools, attached to the floor with steel. The ceiling was about 2.5 meters high. With six 4 foot long fluorescent bulbs. In the center 6 cheap plastic chairs, obviously for us. The 2 M-16 toters followed us on either side of the door. Glancing back at them, I noticed a security type, but high resolution brand, video camera over the door opening. It could swivel. But now, it was pointed center of the far wall, at the general.

There were 2 soldiers standing on each side, one soldier standing on each side of the general. Who was sitting down very relaxed, leaning on his rifle, like it was a staff. Those soldiers also had pistols in their holsters. Their rifles, like the rest of the soldiers that were already in the room, had longer rifles, traditional shaped, M-14s. That were still in inventory, for sorts of special soldiers. But not many. The 2 soldiers who searched us, came in behind us, and the hydraulics started to raise the door.

I almost bolted out the door, even as it was rising. I almost warned JC. M-14s shoot a much bigger bullet. That could be custom loaded, more powder, sharper, Teflon, bullets, to defeat Texas scale armor. Not with much velocity left, but still adequate killing power. Comparable to Jenny's .25 pistol. And I noted that everyone but us was wearing military earmuff hearing aids. Which also work as if good ear plugs. But I did neither. JC knew his weapons, so I didn't want to give away us knowing my telling him. JC seemed calm enough, even happy. So I stood with my chimp comrades.

The general, one star, yelled "AIM!!!" Of course, they were already READY. The chimps reacted to the noise, before it was even a word. The 4 chimp bodyguards grabbed a rifle aimed at them, with one hand, not more than blocking it aside. After all, these were extra large hoomies. The 2 hoomies left and right of the general, separated a little, shooting at JC. Their bullets, along with quite a few others, banged and ricocheted, around the van. I was already, at least, temporary deaf. They were a little slower than they should have been. And JC dodged the first 2 shots apiece. These were some of the best combat, and target shots, in the fed army. They could not help, squeezing, not jerking, the trigger. Why take the extra time to fine tune an aim, when that point will no longer by the intended target? When is close combat with chimps, just keep pointing and jerking. Hopefully, you'll get lucky. (But I wasn't their weapons instructor.)

One of the M-16 toters was trying to get a shot at JC, from the back. But I think JC had seen him out of the corner of his eyes, seconds earlier. JC had a struggling hoomy and chimp between him, before that misaimed shot, missed the general's face by 2 inches. That soldier then concentrated on one of the chimps in the struggle. Having a safe enough, from hitting his comrade, shot, at the wrestling chimp's armor. He knew, that even though the final plastic armor would stop the rest of the M-16 bullet, it would destroy some armor. Soon, the "hardballs", minus the jackets, would penetrate chimp.

I was about to lunge at him, when the other M-16 guy, who spoke to us earlier, pointed his rifle a half meter from my face. He yelled "Freeze Scumbag!!!" (We're all scumbags, to these semi-human automations.) Then almost soothingly, "Relax! Enjoy the show. You're the one we're going to take prisoner." A half second later, flying from out of nowhere, a pistol in its sheath, but torn from some belt, skidded on the floor, a little over 2 meters from me. Now, I had good reason to obey, and I sat down quick. But the speaker guy glanced at it with a raised eyebrow, and gave the "no! no!" sign, with his finger.

By now, things had moved lightning fast. Reminiscent of the fastest few seconds, of the JC v. Buckaroos video. Of the four hoomies wrestling with the chimp bodyguards, one had his eyes, then his throat, ripped out by a chimp's claw. Two had a hand bitten near off. They dropped their rifles, and were backing off, in shock. One's throat was ripped out by chimp teeth and fangs, lying face down, almost dead already, in a pool of blood. 3 chimps leaped snarling at 3 new targets.

The other chimp was on the floor. He had taken 3 hits through the back. Not very disabling M-16 bullets. But a shot thru his shoulder, paralyzed his whole right arm. The speaker guy was one of the new targets. The second he glanced away, I stretched and kicked the pistol. It skidded into the hands of the chimp on the floor. He snatched it up with a <Hoot!> of triumph.

JC had been too busy as the favorite target, to hurt any hoomies. Amazingly, he was unharmed, and only a glancing bullet that hit his armor, and took away several scales. Now, JC was throwing plastic chairs at the general. Who stopped being a military decoration, and was trying to shoot at JC. He got off several shots. But JC was the only one who was not in danger of the bullets. One missed my hand, by 2 feet. Ricocheted twice, and dented my soldier boot, leaving a black bruise on my foot. It seemed like JC had an endless supply of chairs. They bounced around so much, there was always one in reach.

The M-16 guy who threatened me, was now wrestling with a chimp. After 3 shots either missed, or hit the chimp's armor. I hit him with a kara te punch. 2 largest knuckles to the temple. And the big oaf fell like a sack of potatoes, unconscious, twitching and kicking. And the chimp chewed out his throat, before he hit the ground.

The one armed chimp fired 4 shots, that ended the battle. The 4th shoot hit the general in the hand. The general <yelp!>ed dropping his rifle. All the other hoomies were dead. (Unlike hoomies, a chimp CAN grip his pistol well enough one handed, to shoot accurately.) One Arm looked questioningly at JC. JC signed <No.>. I said "Shoot him! Dead." JC signed to me <Why?>. "He's just a one star guy. I'm not in the mood for risking any more of his tricks." JC signaled another chimp that was holding a rifle. <BWANG!!! BWANG!!! BWANG!!!> went 3 more metallic explosively echoing shots. And a dead general.

I was suddenly calm enough to be aware of my environment. I nearly gagged. Nor just the stench. The entire floor was a blood puddle. Dark red blood, starting to coagulate. And even less appetizing things. It seemed waiting for the hatch to open to ooze out. The walls were liberally splashed with blood, too. In few places, the blood was dripping down. It was a wonder, that none hit the camera lense.

I peeled off the smallest soldier uniform. It was very baggy on me. But with luck, now noticeable from 1000 meters off. I explained my plan to JC, as I was doing that. Before we left, I looked, under the table, the desk drawer nearest the camera. Sure enough, the camera was wired to that recorder. And it was on. I popped out the CD ROM and put it into a nice paper container. That was also in the drawer, along with 3 other CD packages, that still had CDs in them. I handed it to a chimp bodyguard, and signed <careful>. My way of handling it, sort of, translated that into <fragile>. I signed <Important> 3 times. Which would translate, sort of, into <Very Important!>. I pressed for the door/ramp to ramp. As soon as there was a large crack, I left on the driver's side. And JC left on the other side carrying a ball peen hammer, a shortsword and a military pistol. He looked like a flash of black fur, going underneath the van.

I walked to the driver's narrow, bullet resistant, window, with a military pistol stuffed on the backside of my belt. And I tapped on the window with my knuckles. "General Crawford wants you to drive us into Bartlesville. He wants me to show you where to go." The driver opened the door, about a 6 inch crack. I shouldered in, holding the pistol with both hands, about a foot from his face, "Hands on your head!" After he opened his mouth in shock for a few seconds, he did so. This was still a tense situation. He had a holstered pistol on his belt, and an M-16 on the floor.

By this time, JC had no problem opening the passenger door. That door was unlocked, too. And he was pointing his pistol at the driver. He raised an eyebrow questioning. I said "Let's not get blood thirsty. He was obviously out of the loop. Or he wouldn't have been so easy. ... Sir, please go back into the van, with JC here, I don't want you to be tempted to try anything heroic. The Command Center's a mess, so don't be shocked." He was walking with JC, before I even finished saying that. At some point, JC removed his pistol belt. Now JC looked like a chimp version of a 2 gun gunslinger. I managed to start the engine, without gunning the accelerator, too bad. I struggled with the unfamiliar stick shift. But I didn't lurch the van too badly, as I turned it around, and drove it thru the Texan side of the confrontation. …

Later. JC slapped me on the shoulder, chattering happily, and started scribbling, <Sorry I had to treat you like that. But you hoomies get cocky when you have the upper hand. I didn't want to trust your acting skills to be perfect. The best at acting ignorant, is someone who is ignorant. It would have been a lot worse, if we hadn't acted first. Even you underestimated me! Remember: The feds only taught me all the close quarter combat THEY knew. These guys are my best Chimp Fu students. Really, shields wouldn't have been much use anyway, in close quarters. They gave themselves away, when they added more restrictions>.

The medics said my hearing would be back to normal, in 2 weeks.

The video and audio CD was on the local, and Dallas TV. stations, before noon. And on about every functional TV. and radio station in the 48 U.S. states, before sunset. And around most of the world, before then.

In around 3 months, "one arm" had almost perfectly good use of his arm back.

This outrage was the final straw, for the Confederacy, Federation Loyalist and Texas. They were mobilizing to blitz the feds. In the face of a sure losing war, few feds were ready to stand by Prez Northwitch. And about half of those were scattered thru out the U.S.A., too few together, to be any effect. And about 500, wouldn't be much defense of Washington D.C. Northwitch demanded that us chimps negotiate with him again. (Yes, he was that delusional, and neurotic, ego maniac. He did demand.) It seemed ☺ very generous of us, agreeing to a meet. But we insisted that it would be in a Holiday Inn room outside of Dallas. Northwitch would be searched, and brought weaponless, and without retainers, to the hotel room.

He Who Sups with The Devil, …

It was a typical hotel room. A bed, living room, and no kitchenette, combined. A small room, with a door, was the bathroom. A once nice, blue carpet covered floor. Rather then give the comedians an opportunity to say, we were in bed together, and to pass a good chance for one-upsmanship; we brought 3 chairs of our own. One was a nice, very comfortable lounge, chair, that no one had any right to complain about. Mine was throne like, to the left. JC's was a big, veritable throne. But because he sat lower "in the saddle" than I do, he was only a half a head "taller" then me. Similar, I would be only a half head "taller" then Prez Northwitch. JC was unarmed. I carried only a military style .45 caliber pistol, in a military style holster.

We also had a 2 man camera team, manning a pro TV. type video camera. (Not the more compact, roving reporter model.) To broadcast thru out the U.S.A., and most of the world. Show time!

Soon a knock on the door. 2 Texas "Militia" soldiers, appeared. With rifles slung on their backs. One opened the door. And Prez Northwitch appeared. "Please shut the door, please." I asked jovially. The soldiers were already on their way. So, Northwitch had to shut the door himself. (Right on camera. ☺) He was a big, portly, man, in a nice 3 piece blue suit. And super expensive Italian shoes of some brand or another. Us three were a strange contrast. With my blue jeans, tennis shoes, and army surplus fatigue shirt, and pistol; I had the not very dedicated guerilla look. JC wore his usual hair suit, and no adornments.

Northwitch looks a lot like Elmer Fudd. And now with his pout lip expression, more than usual. Hence, his popular name. But unlike the cartoon character, he had no sense of honesty, fairness, kindliness nor decency. You could see this man's soul, just by looking at him. Malice neurotic ego delusions and greed. No real redeeming traits, except ambition. That is typical of what was the big leaders among the hoomies. Only very few carried their personalities, and attitudes, "on their shirt sleeves", like Northwitch did. On the contrary, about all they had going for themselves, was suave, and rich-folks-cool. And of course, money that great+ grand dad had stolen or sleazed. The politicians, the CEOs, the movie stars, and ad nauseam. It was sickening how far, a once great, species had fallen. It's a wonder the baboons hadn't conquered us, even without any genetic engineering.

Northwitch thought he'd take the initiative, and keep us off balance, by "forcing" us to speak first. He asked with only a minor note of sarcasm, "What do you want?" Although we made a not entirely convincing show, of JC typing his speech, and they I "translating" it. I really did most of it. He was mainly just the prompter. I had done most of the writing of it. Still, we were a pretty good team.

"First a word from our sponsors! Texas, The Confederacy and the Federated Loyalists. They want a war with China, until there are no Chinese soldiers in the fourty eight states. And we, too, agree!" JC shamelessly played a recording of one of the applause tracks, of one of our football games. And his hooting did nothing for his dignitas. ☺ Northwitch turned red. But managed to contain his anger. His lip was even poutier than before. He said in a huff "We came prepared to concede a more vigorous war effort."

I continued before he could choose a direction, "Of course, there will be no more genocide of chimps. Chimps will have 'Extraterritoriality'. That is, chimps will only be judged by other chimps. And hoomies that commit crimes against chimps, will be judged by chimps. All hoomies and chimps, will obey the chimp nobles. The chimp nobles are graded by rank, highest first, as follows". …

"I, JC, am the Emperor. Generally for life. Succession is by heir, or my choice. As you know Cliff is the Caesar. Which is, now, the second highest rank. It too, is for life, succession is by heredity, or the Caesar's choice. Although chimps have surpassed hoomies as dominant species. We will still have one hoomie Caesar, to demonstrate solidarity, peace and brotherhood, with the hoomies".

"These are the other noble ranks; Consul, Praetor, and Legate. These will be appointed, often for life, by the Emperor. The federal government will pay these nobles, an equal weekly division of their yearly salary. Ten million hours for the Emperor, eight million for the Caesar four million for the Consuls, two million for the Praetors, and one million hours for the Legates. Further more, all chimps on U.S. soil will be henceforth considered U.S. citizens. And with chimp entitlement, to one hundred Hours a week".

"We will also have a special-Consul. Who will always be a hoomie. For the main purpose of helping the hoomies regain their Space Faring Destiny. Besides his Consul salary. He will be the sole owner of NASA. I am proud and happy to announce, that the first Special Consul – will be the Cliff-friend Hiro!"

"By the way. I know there is a war going on. But we insist that the fed government spend at least ten million hours a month on NASA. ... Anything you want to discuss?!"

Northwitch sputtered (probably and act, or exaggeration). "Do you really think the American people will stand for this!?!" "Of course they will! You've bred, cowed and wage-slaved them to be subservient, cowardly, drug and booze sotted slobs. They know that following us is their best path to regaining their worth as sentient species. Not to mention their space Faring destiny. They know we'll govern a lot better, cheaper and nicer, than your kind will. JC could be elected prez, and nobody would oppose him, and suffer the embarrassing landslide. ... Speaking of such things!"

"Two weeks from today, all elected fed officers, and a list of others we will announce, will resign from office. They will be replaced by our temporary appointments. To maintain the government and prepare for very soon, truly fair, not rigged elections. The DemocraticRepublican party is now outlawed. Whose members cannot meet, nor run, nor hold, any political office or appointment. As they have proven themselves both enemies of democracy. And violent, criminal, militant enemies of the U.S. Constitution."

"We hope, as these reforms are implemented. That the different factions will rejoin the fed government, as described in the U.S. Constitution. However, we reaffirm states' rights to succeed from the union. And frankly, we have little hope that Texas will join us. After all, they are doing VERY well without us." I paused in silence to let the effect sink in. For the camera. After all, Prez Northwitch was just a goofy "sounding board", to lend us authority. ☺

Northwitch snarled, "Why don't you just take the space program too!" "Because you hoomies are more advanced. And us chimps just aren't suited for the great space base, the moon. On the moon trees and orchards are extremely un-practical. We'll share Mars and Venus with you, when they're terraformed. Maybe some of the other moons, if they prove chimp habitable enough." This was getting off track, but we might as well share our vision of the future with the camera, while were at it.

Northwitch opined, "It won't take you so long to catch up, especially with hoomy slaves, as you call us. Then you could have the whole space program." I replied "Whether you like it or not. All on this planet are in it together. Look at you! All of your ilk think that you are oh-so-. tough. But look how close to the skin surface you're jugular vein is. Us chimps aren't all that tough. But you hoomies are pathetic. Obviously something has made you to be exceptionally easy to kill, compared to all other animals. A bobcat could kill you. For that matter, if a 3 kilo kitten cat was aggressive enough, it could give you a very good fight. You've been both selectively bred, and genetically engineered, to be what you are. Just what an interstellar species would want, to occupy this planet. Easy to kill, cooperative and intelligent. You weren't all that different from us chimps, when around 150 of you left Africa, to populate the rest of the world. If the other space faring species are not friendly. You will certainly need us."

Northwitch, in high pout lipped dudgeon, retorted with icy sarcasm "Well! If that's ALL?! I will report back your Directives to my cabinet and Congress." "No! I have two more items before we adjourn. One. We charge you with thousands of counts of genocide, against chimps. Although we believe there should be a general amnesty, ending this second, for genocide against chimps. Because most who have done the actual killing, were ordered by people such as yourself. And bad things happen in war. And we wouldn't want everyone to think that we are spoiled sport winners. But. We think you, Supreme Commander, should be made an example.

"Two. We charge you with attempted murders. Concerning your recent attack on six of us, who were under protection of peace conference truce. What do you have to say in your defense?"

Northwitch glowered, and there was the low growl of an angry dog in his voice, "It is the right and duty, of every human, to slay you, monsters! Anyway we can! As you just announced, you are trying to take over the world." "Hmmm. It seems that we don't even have as much rights as kangaroo rats, and spotted owls? No. Never mind!

That was just a rhetorical question. I find you guilty of all counts. And I will pass sentence in a few seconds."

I drew and fired my .45 in one smooth motion, into a modified sitting version of the weaver stance. <WHOOM!> This time, I was wearing my earplugs. It smashed a hole, almost exactly center of Northwitch's forehead. Splattering brains, blood and icor all over the floor. For a few seconds Northwitch stood still, no change of expression, like he couldn't believe there was a hole in his head. Then he started jerking, and spasming, as he slid to the floor. "Let's get out of here!", I said.

AND THEY ALL LIVED HAPPILY EVER AFTER, UNLESS I WRITE A SEQUEL.

We were in a hurry. Although we were in Texas, "He needed killing" is a popular, and sometimes successful, murder defense. I sure wasn't going to risk it, with the political maelstrom, we just caused.

I already chartered a civilian armor clad, to take me to the Dothan Alabama airport. Where British Airlines had just established 2 flights a day to Europe. JC rode with me, to Baton Rouge, where he caught a ride to, where he didn't say.

10 or so miles over the Texas-Louisiana border, we stopped in front of a café, where our driver, and shotgun guard, knew a pretty waitress. We weren't in the mood for a meal stop, especially a greasy spoon. So I and JC went to a convenience store, that had a big sign "Non-Texas Colas Sold Here". If you've ever drank a texacola, you know why! This gave us some privacy. ...

Walking there, I suggested to JC; "Why don't you live in big luxurious tents, like the Mongol Hoarders? And command things by phone. Out in a nice wilderness, with plenty of supplies dropped in by helicopter. That would be safe and fun." He wrote on his new mini computer display <That's a great idea Cliff! So that's what I am going to have my double do. What I am going to do, is smuggle myself, and a few extra comrades, to Africa. I'm going to liberate my oppressed brothers in Africa! Want to come along?> "No thanks. I'm going to stay out of wars for a while. But it is a good idea. If we take all of sub-Sahara Africa, we will be able to build a population that rivals the hoomies. A good first step toward breeding them out of control of the planet. Eventually, we'll have to force them to reduce theirs population to a max of one billion. So we can clean up this planet. I suggest following the advice of Sun Tsu Set, as and try to win Africa without a military battle" <Shhhhhh! Don't tell my soldier-chimps that. To make them feel useful, we will have to make it look like a war.> …

"If each owns a nice mansion castle. I'm sure they'll manage to fit into a peaceful society." <If each hoomy had a mansion castle, even they'd be civilized, too. ☺> …

Soon after I entered Alabama. I got a call on my e-phone. "Cliff, it's me Laverne!" "How did you get this number?!" "It wasn't easy. <giggle!> I've managed to restart your chimp farm. But it's an all volunteer thing, now. And some of the chimps want to restart your teams. But we're going to have to renegotiate my salary. And my back pay. <Giggle!> I've been putting in a LOT of hours. And U.S. dollars are no good anymore." <Giggle!> "Tell you what. I'll just sign over the farm and the teams, and let you deal with it. I'll give you whatever Hours you need, to get you going. Maybe, when I get back, I'll start up one of those Bloodbowl teams, and an Urban Brawl team. But right now, I don't want to do anything but fly around the world, and do nothing productive, at all. Say! I bet the New U.S. government will want you, as an ambassador to the Chimp Nation. And I'd bet a lot of colleges would want you as Dean of some college, or another." …

When I stepped in the departure line, at the airport. Jenny, my main squeeze from the Hide Out, grabbed me in a big hug, out of nowhere. And said "Hi! My master JC said he wants you to keep me for a while." She turned pink, as she whispered "He wants to breed me with you." I'd been wondering what happened to her, after I left the Hide Out, to "negotiate" with that general, Crawford. "Tell JC that traditionally I get the pick of the litter." I meant it as sarcastic humor. But she took it the wrong way. "That's sweet of you!" she cooed.

Hmmmm. Maybe I'd just pay a team of child sitters, and scientists, to raise her kid as intensely educated as JC was. If we were better raised, and much better bred, than we were doing now. Then maybe we'd equal or surpass the chimps, yet. And if Hiro ever actually gets his telepathy together, we might once again have something the chimps, lack. And once we regain the lost genetic engineering tech. … She started kissing my face and whispering, "You know. JC really wants you to keep me. We can't have babies. And he likes chimpettes better." "Why doesn't he want you around, just for fun, every once in a while?" She turned pink again and whispered "He said something about, it's like throwing a hot dog down the hall way." I couldn't help getting a puffed up ego, from that.

For a while, other passengers were taking advantage, and walking past us. Until an old lady was behind us, and kept nudging us along. Although Jenny was still as pretty and curvaceous as ever. There were good reasons not to mess with her. The main reason, because I already had her. But she was fun, and easy to get rid of. Now we were at the boarding platform. And didn't have to ask, to know she had no ticket. I said to the ticket handler, as I handed him my ticket, "This lady is with me. I am the Caesar." …

It's good to be the Caesar!

Finis.

Printed in the United States
By Bookmasters